Comhairle Contae
Átha Cliath Theas
South Dublin County Council

D0120379

We Germans

We Germans

Alexander Starritt

JM ORIGINALS

First published in Great Britain in 2020 by JM Originals
An imprint of John Murray (Publishers)
An Hachette UK company

1

A CIP catalogue record for this title is available from the British Library

Hardback ISBN 9781529317244
Trade Paperback ISBN 9781529343533
eBook ISBN 9781529317268

Typeset in Adobe Garamond 12.25/16.25 pt by
Palimpsest Book Production Limited, Falkirk, Stirlingshire

Printed and bound in Great Britain by Clays Ltd, Elcograf S.p.A.

John Murray policy is to use papers that are natural, renewable and
recyclable products and made from wood grown in sustainable forests.
The logging and manufacturing processes are expected to conform to
the environmental regulations of the country of origin.

John Murray (Publishers)
Carmelite House
50 Victoria Embankment
London EC4Y 0DZ

www.johnmurraypress.co.uk

In memory of my beloved grandparents,
Walter and Katharina Pretzsch

My dear Callum,

It's now been seventeen months since we last saw each other; I hope very much that we'll see each other at least once more. I know you're busy, but come and visit. Whenever suits you – just try to remember to let me know a couple of weeks in advance so I can arrange myself.

I also hope very much that you're not put off by the conversation we had when you were here. It didn't occur to me at the time, but I've since started to think that maybe you would be feeling guilty. But then we've never telephoned that much anyway, so who knows. In any case, it doesn't matter.

I don't want to make you feel worse, but I did understand what you were trying to do: hear my stories about Russia before I get too addled to tell them. It's not a happy thing to realise, and I admit that it irritated me. But on reflection I can see that your thinking was right: I *am* at an age when people tilt very quickly towards – shall we just say, towards a place where people tell no stories.

Your questions were ridiculous, though – awkward, faux naïve. You should have seen yourself edging up backwards to what you really wanted to ask: did you see terrible things? Let me answer that for you now: yes, I did. And: did you *do* terrible things? It's hard to say, but certainly not in the way you presume.

What surprises me is this: do you imagine that your mother didn't ask the same questions when she was your age? Or that they haven't kept resurfacing, like chunks in soup, ever since I came back? Your mother's generation were less polite about it. And rightly so, I should emphasise. Those aren't polite questions.

But even if I'd wanted to give you a proper answer when you were here, I wouldn't have been able to. You have to understand that even experiences that extreme don't stay sharp in the mind for ever.

What you end up doing, what I ended up doing, is finding some phrases that simplify eventful years down to something that can be said over coffee, and then you remember that phrase instead of the silent figures who stand behind it. I've tended to say that it was a cruel time to be alive, but that some people, as we all know, had it much, much worse. And that we should be grateful our times are so peaceful now.

The reason for developing these platitudes is as feeble and mundane as not wanting to think about the 1940s every day. Like anyone else, you want some coffee and conversation about something pleasant – maybe even more than other people would. If we who lived through it do talk about it, and we do more and more now that we're old, we talk about Hitler and world history instead of about ourselves. I sometimes think my wine circle sounds like a group of petitioners each trying to get a two-line amendment into history's verdict.

So when you gave me your clumsy interview, nothing from those years occurred to me as quickly as it would have needed to. By the time I was thinking about it, rather than about how angry you'd made me, you'd already left again and were back in London, living your life and perhaps forgetting all about this conversation with your grandfather.

I, on the other hand, have more time than I know what to do with. That is, if you measure in days and not years. It recently struck me again how young your oma was when she died. Seventy-two! I hardly even know anyone that young any more, apart from my family and the people who work here. I really thought we'd have longer together.

But anyway: lots of time, lots of quiet and nothing to do. And my memory, once you'd kicked it, began, slowly, wheezily at first, to turn over.

With very old memories, it seems that the more you roll them around, the more they pick up. Faces I hadn't seen in decades now appear among the other diners in the restaurant, and I catch the whisper of forgotten names in the chatter at the bakery. Of everything, it's the people who come back first. Sometimes it's not unlike a reunion. Many I'm happy to see again.

Then come sounds and sensations, more and more of them. The motorised snorting from the gun carriage I drove into Russia on. The hunger – my goodness I remember the hunger, when it's in your arms and legs, as if you can actually feel the muscle cells breaking down. Just the memory of it was enough to send me to the Greek's for a plate of souvlaki and chips, more than I could ordinarily hope to finish. I knew what I was doing, of course, but it was reassuring to be able to do it.

These mundanities are probably not what you wanted to hear about, but this is what there is. Since our conversation, I've felt again the constant mild sunburn, the tight aching skin on my forearms and the back of my neck, in that first Ukrainian summer. The thick, standing heat that I loved and that lay on us like gravy – we'd string poncho canopies across the back of the gun carriage and doze in the shade, stripped to our underclothes, while we jolted through the countryside. The coppery dust churned up from the dirt roads would stick to us while we daydreamed, and if you didn't find a river to jump in, you'd have to scrape it off as red paste in the evenings.

As these sense-memories have come back from the brink of oblivion, they've started stretching out towards each other, joining up and thickening into incidents, conversations, things that happened. The more I write down, the more there is. An old burn on the back of my left hand has begun to itch again. It wasn't all sunbathing. I heard shellfire the other day while I was walking in the park, the dull thump of my howitzer. And just this morning, in the lift, I suddenly found myself running a sweat, my face purple, my heart in the grip of a fear that had long been dormant.

It's all made me think that perhaps I can *do* something with this time I still have. The plan was that your oma and I would be travelling and enjoying our retirement. Well, life isn't fair, we know that. There you go: another platitude. But can you imagine what she'd say if she knew I'd been watching television in the afternoons?

I know she'd be pleased to think of me using the energy and lucidity I have left. Working again, after all those years of working towards being able to stop. It feels good. She'd be pleased whatever I was doing, but you were always her favourite; she'd be happy I'm doing something for you, even if it's only writing you this long letter.

I read somewhere that in medieval Japan old samurai used to write down what they'd learned about how to live, to help educate their sons and grandsons. Each generation added their own experiences, so that as a young man you could be handed the advice of centuries. I've always liked that idea. Especially because I wish you and my father could have met. He was a reader, the bookish kind of minister, who decorated his house with shelves. I think you would have liked each other.

And there's something about my time in the East that I want to explain to you. I can't quite articulate it myself. And I don't want you to jump to the pantomime conclusion: it's not that I have some confessions to get off my chest before the end. I'm not trying to clear my conscience. What's on it is on it.

I wasn't a Nazi. No court would find me guilty of anything, even an omniscient one. What I want to tell you isn't about atrocities or genocide. I didn't see the camps and I'm not qualified to say anything about them. I read Primo Levi's book about it, the same as everyone else. Except of course that when we Germans read it, we have to think: We did this.

But this isn't about that. What I want to tell you about is something quite different. It's to do with courage. I don't think anyone who sees real courage ever forgets it, I suppose because it's so unlike anything else in our characters. It's as bright in my mind now as if I were again lying in that scrubby Polish field long ago, with an appalling man named Lüttke lying on top of me.

I saw it in war, in captivity and once, years later, in peacetime: after your uncle Jochen came back from the hospital, his friends, who didn't know his leg had been amputated, knocked on the door downstairs and asked whether he wanted to play football. He was a child, a terminally ill child, and he could have just turned over in his bed. I think your oma wanted him to.

But he went outside and played football with them on his crutches in the yard behind the house. And didn't just play – and fall over – but laughed and shouted and was happy. That's courage. And I have not forgotten it.

~

CALLUM EMSLIE: I'm not sure exactly what kind of disease my uncle Jochen had, just that it was in the bone marrow in his leg and that he died the day he turned twelve, in 1968. He'd clung on to see his birthday. That story of him playing football on his crutches I've heard from at least four people: my grandparents, my mum and one of the other boys, who's since become a mildly creepy evangelical Christian. He retold it to me at my opa's funeral, about half a century after the game.

It's true that I asked my opa some less than tactful questions on that visit. And as for that guilt trip about seeing him at least once more, yes, I saw him a bunch more times. I may not have been a gold-standard grandson, but I think I did alright. It wasn't like he lived down the street: his flat was on this domesticated wooded hill outside Heidelberg, in the easy-going, wine-producing south-west of Germany. I went every summer when I was a kid. Even when I was a student and in my cash-strapped twenties, I forked out for the flights every couple of years, which at the time I thought was often enough. As I get older I think more about how alone he must have been.

But I liked going. I admired him, basically for being so unimaginably stoic. A few years before he died, he was walking in the woods by himself and had some kind of leg spasm. He must have gone down in a heap and couldn't get back up. There was no one about, so he dragged himself arm over arm back to the road to find help, and then tried to pretend it hadn't been a big deal. That was what he was like, and that was when he was nearly ninety.

In all the times I saw him after this conversation, he never mentioned the long letter he was writing. Presumably he finished writing it after a while and put it in a drawer: when he died, my other uncle found it among his things, addressed to me. That was only a brief year or so before my wife and I first got together – I often think how close the two of them were to overlapping.

My opa had actually started writing a memoir once before, soon after my oma died. It had nothing to say about the war or his time in captivity, but started on the day he and my oma met, when he got back to Germany. It was mainly about holidays they'd been on, their kids' birthday parties, happy days. He gave up on it when his grief took a different turn. He had to live a long time without her.

That visit when I asked him about Russia, I'd assumed he'd be keen to talk. From my late teens to my mid-twenties, whenever I was telling him about reading French and German at university or getting my first paying jobs in TV afterwards, he'd say something like, 'When I was your age, I was in a trench outside Donetsk' or 'I was just starting my second year in the Gulag.' The lesson was simple: don't forget how lucky you are to have been born when you were.

I thought that if for once I dared ask directly about it, laptop recorder poised, I'd get hours of powerful oral history. I imagined that I could play the recording to future generations and say, This is the voice of your great-great-grandfather. Pretty moving stuff, I'm sure you'll agree. But, as he says, nothing came of it. The only bit I remember is that, hoping to prompt a colourful story of hardship in the Gulag, I asked what the Russians had given him to eat. He considered for a while and then told me, 'I suppose it will have been some kind of soup.'

So even though I've put in notes to clarify anything that would be obscure to non-Germans, the background I can add is meagre: he was conscripted out of school into the Wehrmacht in 1940, helped invade the Soviet Union in 1941, fought in the artillery on the Eastern Front for four years, was captured in what is now Austria in 1945 and sent to a Russian prison camp north-east of the Black Sea, where he was kept until 1948. That doesn't tell you much.

~

The events I want to tell you about happened in late 1944, when the war was almost fully lost and our mental, physical and moral disintegration almost complete.

A few years earlier, we'd gone East as a mechanised modern army of tanks, lorries, gun carriages, field kitchens and mobile smithies, less like soldiers than mechanics, professional and specialised, our ears numbed by the engines, our hands and faces smeared with oil, the air around us thick and sweet with petrol. Our task was simply to keep the great steel machine rolling East – always East, going deeper and deeper, through Polish forests and Ukrainian cornfields and Russian towns and villages and cities, endlessly.

Proud and confident, wearing our laurels as the conquerors of Poland and France, we drove into the Eastern vastness and were destroyed there. By 1944, those of us still alive were fleeing on foot, broken, bedraggled, our tanks blown up, our artillery abandoned, our good name blackened for generations, our friends and brothers-in-arms buried in hostile soil.

Our fall was from a very great height. In that first, victorious summer, our invading tanks covered half the distance to St Petersburg in five days. Five days! The limiting factor on our speed wasn't the Red Army, but the road surface: mud rather than tarmac. I remember my gun commander telling me, We're going to win this war with a hopsa, heissa, tralala.

On the back of my gun carriage, I rode along and daydreamed. While the countryside trundled by or we waited in traffic between undulating cornfields, I'd shave

9

or write self-importantly in my war diary or try to study the first-year chemistry textbooks I'd brought along in case I was back by the next semester.

Artillerymen tended to be more educated than the infantry, and someone in our company had packed an old Baedeker guide to Russia. It must have been written before the Revolution, and its cover had been wrapped in tape to protect it on the journey. But we used it to plan which pictures we'd see in the Hermitage if it hadn't been evacuated by the time we arrived. Grander men than me, who had friends of friends in St Petersburg, were writing home to ask for letters of introduction to people in the city.

I wasn't very worried about Russia. Only in some moments did I get a sense of the danger we were in, something none of us had really understood. When we crossed the Memel, the frontier river in the 'Deutschlandlied' [Callum: Now called the Neman, it divides Lithuania from Russia's Kaliningrad enclave], someone read the description from *War and Peace* of Napoleon's army invading over the same river. Even amid our noisy, mechanised hubris, we heard the echo. And sometimes we'd talk, with a fearful thrill, about the Grande Armée melting into nothing on the long walk home from Moscow.

But I didn't foresee our own catastrophe. None of us did. My main worry was that I wouldn't be released back to university after the Red Army had capitulated. I didn't want to waste years in uniform while the Wehrmacht turned south through the Caucasus to the British oilfields in Iraq, or through Afghanistan and over the Khyber Pass into India.

That seems fantastical now, even deluded. In 1941, it

fitted the facts. The miracle of the six-week victory over France, which in those days was still called 'the ancestral enemy', made us think that the German Army was too advanced, too strategically sophisticated, to be seriously opposed by what we imagined as a horde of illiterate serfs.

Our fathers and uncles had suffered here and in France for four years, and lost; this time, with the invention of the Blitzkrieg, we thought we'd graduated to a higher plane of warfare; that German industry and organisation, and German standards of training and professionalism, even among the rank and file, were matchless. But invading Russia was like declaring war on the sea; it just swallowed us.

I became a pedestrian one day in spring 1943, in the eastern part of Ukraine, more than a thousand kilometres from the German border. The same terrifying thing had happened that kept happening on the long retreat: the Russians had overrun our flanks and were trying to encircle us. We had to race them West, to get past the point where their two pincers were going to meet.

Our panicky column got jammed on the dirt track, with the road blocked by lorries, tanks and staff cars trying to get past each other. It was almost night but we had no headlamps on, and everyone kept driving into each other. On both sides of the road were the burning hulls of ve-hicles hit by Russian planes and rammed out of the way.

Ahead we could see the red sun declining into the West; along the dark horizon behind we could see the sky flick-ering as shells landed at our rear; all around us, in the ditches and the fields, whole or in pieces, were dead Germans.

The blockage was because of a steep incline in the road, part of some raised ground we were supposed to regroup on. It can't have been more than a couple of hundred metres, and on a tarmacked road in a modern car you probably wouldn't even change gear to go over it. But it had rained earlier and the road surface had melted into a kind of red, sticky, tenacious clay. Each time a lorry's tyres made a half-turn, the treads acted like the buckets on a waterwheel, bringing up clay to the gap between the wheel and the arch, where it started to set.

Some of us were pulling the clay out in handfuls. A lorry shifted forward in the confusion and snapped someone's arm. No one went to help him. A team of soldiers wedged horizontal poles into a lorry's chassis, like oars, and, while the engine turned as slowly as possible, they tried to help push it up the slope. The further up they got, the deeper the lorry sank into the wet clay, until the poles were level with their knees. Eventually, the wheels locked. Then the whole heavy contraption started to slide backwards down the hill into the queue behind.

There was a corpse who'd got stuck in the clay at the bottom of the slope, one of ours, a German. No one had the time or leisure to drag him out, and every time the lorry went back and forth over his sunken legs, it levered his stiff torso up off the ground. Back and forth, and each time the split grey face and the battered torso rising from the mud. I remember thinking, We are in hell. This is hell and we are the damned. Someone has decided that our punishment can't wait till we're dead, and hell has risen to spread itself across this twilit Ukrainian countryside. We must get out.

The shellfire on our rear was getting closer and the Russians were starting to land salvoes of Katyusha rockets in flurries of shrieks and whumps. The column ran out of patience with the lorry. A furious, shaking staff officer with muddy handprints on his red-striped trousers screamed for the soldiers to get out of the way. He told a tank to get up there on its caterpillar tracks, and he kept saying to everyone around him, At least we can save the tanks.

The tank jerked forward, trying to build up speed, and ground the trapped corpse into the road. The steel tracks got further up the little incline than the lorry had, but soon it, too, started to clog and slow. Finally it reached a high point and then began to slide backwards, slipping off centre as it came back down. When it hit the waiting traffic, it was going fast enough to crush part of the lorry that the staff officer was standing on. The officer looked at the wrecked lorry and his wrecked legs, fumbled his pistol out of its holster and shot himself in the temple.

At that point we abandoned everything. The heavy guns, the transport, the tanks we needed to defend ourselves – we poured the last of our petrol over them and set them on fire.

Despair, yes, bitter pain and disappointment, but also a strange angry relief in sloshing petrol across the only things that would ever get us out of Russia and home. As we flicked matches onto petrol-soaked seats and into flatbeds, the army lost some of its power over us. Eat now, sleep now, march now, follow your leader – that's what they'd demanded of us; we'd followed, and they'd led us into disaster.

Usually everything was about we, us, the company, the army, but as we took our revenge on the machines that had carried us here, I thought: I never asked to be here, in this uniform or this godforsaken country.

I was furious that my life had been wasted, that I was going to die on some Ukrainian roadside for nothing. I had done as I was told, I had postponed my studies and my desire to become a great scientist, and this was what they'd used me for.

Amid the rising firelight and the oily billows of smoke, there was some release. After all, what could the army do to us that would be worse than the Russians, with the war unwinnable, the initiative lost, the retreat practically endless.

But after we'd burned our heavy equipment, we carried on fighting, on foot, for years. Hope, discipline, loyalty, the will to survive – I don't know what got us up every morning, maybe just habit and a narrowness of thought. Perhaps simply fear of what the Russians would do to us if we didn't stick together.

A lot of fighting in an army doesn't entail the violence of two people trying to hurt each other. Most of it is communication, logistics, learned routines. Apart from some rare, specific situations, where you're in touching range of the other side, you don't need to be an aggressive person to be a good soldier.

So I 'fought', yes, but did so mainly by digging holes, firing my rifle, using my experience to improve the layout of our positions. I stayed practical. At school I'd often been top of my class; my whole upbringing predisposed me to diligence, attentiveness, not just doing the work I'd been set, but putting some thought into how to do it best.

Then sometimes the forwardmost troops in the Russians' pincer movements would manage to meet in front of our retreat. We'd have to rush through them before they could reinforce their line. That was violence, savagery. It made you understand how the very first war must have been: bared teeth, screaming, men hacking at each other with stone tools.

By the time I want to tell you about, autumn 1944, I had fought and retreated like that, with vehicles and without, for two and a half years, across hundreds of kilometres of Russia, of Ukraine and of Poland. Those of us left were close to the German border. Why we didn't all desert right then, strip off the uniforms and slink back to our families, like the Italians or Romanians did, and save millions of lives; why we dug trenches and counter-advanced and kept going until our home towns looked like Warsaw or Stalingrad . . . it's not a question I can really answer.

The idea that we did it merely out of habit, out of misplaced diligence – that path of thought leads up to a moral abyss. But there is some truth in it. Perhaps there was also the remnant of some primitive creed that told us it was better to fight than to capitulate. Perhaps it was a meeting of fear and pride; we couldn't stop without giving up an idea of ourselves.

If we'd rationally wanted to save as many of ourselves as possible, we'd have surrendered in summer 1942. It was often said that we had to defend our people against the

Russians' revenge for what we had done to them. But even when we'd been forced all the way back to fighting in German towns, no one did anything for the civilians we were supposedly trying to protect. They weren't allowed to retreat either, and had to try and save themselves.

It seems incredible now, but right at the end Hitler really did give the so-called Nero order, to dynamite the remaining bridges and factories, poison the water, burn all supplies, destroy anything of value. Only then, in the last few days, when Hamburg, Dresden, Frankfurt, Berlin each looked like a brickmaker's yard, did our ruinous pride finally break.

One day that autumn, a rumour sprang up that a food depot, stocked with French wine, Italian sardines and other loot shipped from the occupied countries for the general staff, was going to be left to the Russians.

Overall, the army's policy was to be like good picnickers, and leave nothing behind. When the Russians advanced, they were supposed to find themselves only ever crossing scorched earth. If our retreats were orderly, we'd lever up railway tracks, throw corpses in the wells, use grenades on the farm machinery. In the normal run of things a depot like this would be doused in petrol and incinerated.

But we were hungry. And our discipline had been loosened by defeat. Our enforced respect for the general staff, never strongly felt, had been turning to resentment since they'd lost the legitimacy of success.

Once – this was still in the early days – I'd seen a high-spirited group of staff officers eat lunch while soldiers dug a trench in front of them. We were outside a village the Russians had fortified and we were waiting for our tanks to come up. While we dug positions and estimated distances, these combed-hair aristocrats had a table set: a white cloth blazing in the sunshine, silver cutlery, sparkling steel buckets filled with ice, and a chef in check trousers to fry their steaks. They had a big map of the area that they spread across the table and weighted down with glasses of white wine. The cold glasses sweated in the sun; we sweated too and watched them and waited to advance into the Russians' arcs of fire.

That's the reality of things, I suppose. There's no reason to think they were bad men, or bad at their work. Generally, I think, the tone of the Wehrmacht was less hierarchical than our allies' armies. But still, it was a speech day for our in-house Communists.

And a general staff food depot we imagined as high-piled strongrooms of edible treasure: luxuries, delicacies, the foods of childhood. After years of subsistence rations, of cabbage and millet, you can imagine what effect this rumour had on us. Heads lifted. Eyes gleamed greedily. People who'd been apathetic for weeks rediscovered their interest in being alive. The chronically hungry veer between apathy and irritation; it wasn't long before some tipped over into anger that this food was about to be abandoned.

For my part, I tried to resist putting any faith in the rumour, which was one of multitudes. Illiterates in the Dark Ages can't have discussed their miracles with more fervour than we discussed ours: the Americans were going to switch sides against the Bolsheviks; Hitler had died of a drug overdose and Himmler was going to negotiate a peace; a coup was about to begin in Moscow. And as the Russians drove us ever closer to Berlin, the miracles had to keep getting more miraculous.

I tried to stay apart from the rumours because I couldn't afford to waste any mental strength absorbing an inevitable disillusionment. And it hurt to admit that other endings for the war were still possible.

I tried not to believe in this depot either.

But in times of desperation a person needs something to hope for. And as my hopes had become more confined, they'd grown more intense, as if the same need were being forced through a smaller hole. So I thought sceptical thoughts about this Aladdin's cave, but hope kept breaking through.

I think our company captain felt the same way. He decided to commit as many of us as he could spare to the search, and started forming groups. Someone asked what we should do if we were caught plundering what was, after all, a Wehrmacht storehouse. The captain told us we should just say we were foraging. That was a concept we were used to, and we wanted him to be right, so we didn't question it.

In my search party, there were four others, none of whom I knew particularly. The specialised branches – artillerymen like me, sappers, signalmen, tankers, all the vaunted professionalism that was supposed to defeat the Eastern hordes – had been minced down and lumped together into a shapeless blob of infantry. In the foxholes beside me were security guards, army bookkeepers, personal aides.

As we were ever more finely chopped, we became more

interchangeable to one another. That suited me. I did not want to know the characters and personal histories of those about to die. Our attrition rate was so high by then that even old *Frontschweine* ['front pigs', i.e. old hands] like me were going every day. The new arrivals came and went like deliverymen, dropping off their own bodies.

And this increasing anonymity made it easier for me to preserve a tiny bright enclave of inner life. To this search party I was simply Oberkanonier Meissner, a man in uniform who did what he was asked, ate his ration and rarely spoke about anything except the task at hand. On the inside, truth be told, I'd become little different.

But there was a buried part of me that remembered my family and held very tight to the determination that if I survived the war I would become a scientist. I could no longer have said why I wanted to, or recalled anything about the chemistry I wanted to study, but it was a talisman: I would not be a soldier for ever.

As it was, I and the other four men in my foraging party looked less like soldiers of the German Army than a band of tinkers fallen on hard times. We were in a motley of ripped clothes, whether issued or pilfered, and carried a hotchpotch of weapons, the most prized being a sturdy Russian sub-machine gun called a papasha. I was wearing a pair of tatty blue Luftwaffe trousers I'd been given in the field hospital when I had Volhynian fever. Every officer who noticed them seemed to consider these wrong trousers a sign that the Wehrmacht really was doomed.

Our messy facial hair made us look like castaways. I had a patch of itchy black stuff thickening around my mouth and straggling up towards my ears. One of the others, Ottermann, the one with the papasha, had a full blond beard, thick and matted, with the tips knotted into two grubby plaits, like a Viking's.

Another, Lüttke, had the huge imperial moustache and mutton chops of a man several decades older, around which the stubble was growing out. He must have been the most insufferable person I met in the whole war – a lickspittle to every passing sergeant and a keen enforcer of any rule that wasn't directed at him.

He'd decked himself out in a mangy black cloak of the kind taken from the corpses of Romanian officers. This absurd garment trailed a sour reek of human decay that made people refuse to sleep near him, but Lüttke was ostentatiously proud of it nevertheless. I think he truly believed the complainers were jealous.

Above this cloak he wore his steel helmet. Rifle strap over one shoulder. And below the cloak he had a pair of valenki – the Eastern-style felt boots that were invaluable in winter but that rotted on your feet and came apart in patches. It wasn't yet cold, so his feet must have been pickling in their own brine.

He was usually being followed around by some frightened recruit. These fresh arrivals were disoriented and close to death, and Lüttke exploited his thin sliver of seniority to have them fetch him water, darn his uniform and give him a tithe of their rations for the privilege. Sometimes he'd be caught by an officer who was still humane enough to mind, and he would grovel cravenly while being rebuked. But by then the army was only just holding together and, short of shooting him, there was little they could do to stop his abuses.

Some officers also seemed to have a wary sense that Lüttke was useful, because he was a sentimentalist. On the occasions when we had a radio to listen to, and they were broadcasting music for the troops, Lüttke would be singing and swaying a hand as if conducting a raucous beer hall. When he didn't know the words, he'd just sing bum-bum-bum, tra-la-la-la-la. These officers seemed to believe it was better for morale than nothing; it probably was.

His stock was high right then because he'd succeeded in stealing a pony. Some acquisitive petty-bourgeois instinct had led him to the copse at the bottom of a field, where he'd found a rickety shed and hidden within it this animal that became the company's pet for a week or so. It was one of the tough, stocky, deep-keeled beasts that pulled the wooden *panje* wagons we used for transport. He was phlegmatic, dun-coloured, with ears like kneadable carpet, and we didn't eat him but named him Ferdy, or Ferdinand [the German for horse is pronounced *ferd*].

We didn't have any machine guns or mortars left for Ferdinand to haul, and he was too barrel-shaped to ride properly, so he carried our backpacks and water flasks – light duties for a *panje* pony. The people who knew about horses competed to assure everyone else that Ferdinand was extremely content. In the time we had him, the company took extra watches at night so that no one could re-steal him from us. And I was glad that, since Lüttke owned him and led him around on a short length of rope, Ferdinand joined our search party.

The captain had marked out sectors on a map for each group, so that our efforts would be systematic. But nobody believed that the other search parties, if they found this depot, would bring anything back for the others. So Lüttke and Ottermann decided we should ignore the instructions and go where we thought the food would be. This, I thought, is how armies disintegrate: we all search for ourselves and no one finds a thing.

But I wanted those loaves of black bread, those venison steaks, that *Apfelkuchen* I was imagining, as much as anyone else. So I joined in as we teased apart the details of the rumour, made some inferences and from this rubbish derived a confident assertion that the depot would be near a village we'd seen on the captain's map.

There was no officer among us and Lüttke, in his rotting Romanian cloak, tried to appoint himself leader. In the middle of the catastrophe, he was angling for promotion to *Unteroffizier*. When we told him we had no intention of wasting our time by acknowledging him as 'operational commander', he acted as if good commanders listen to their men and started leading Ferdinand in the direction we'd agreed.

With his cloak, his pony and his rotting boots, he might have wandered out of the Middle Ages. We followed after him, a gaggle of small, slow figures setting off into a melancholy landscape, looking for a mirage.

The 'foraging' we intended usually meant taking food from the local farms, something we did all the time. There was no other option. Even though nine-tenths of an army's work is moving things from one place to another, it's practically impossible to transport enough bread and soup to—

Ach.

My dear boy, these are horse apples [bullshit] I'm feeding you. The reflex of self-justification. This 'foraging', there's no way around it – it was a crime. A painful thing to write. Not as painful for you as it was for the Russians, I can hear you think. And that's true.

In the East – it was different in France or Norway – but in the East the army's plan for feeding the troops was to 'live off the land', which meant that the people already living off it starved. I don't know anything about how those organisational decisions were made, about policies. I'm not a historian. But these things set the conditions within which we lived well or badly.

What I personally remember is that in the black pre-morning of our opening act of war, with our high-pitched, sleepless exhilaration and the earth-shaking ratsch-bumm, ratsch-bumm of our first real barrage, as we hurried nervously through our training routines of loading and firing, launching our shells into the warm summer night and watching the fires spring up a few seconds later in Soviet Poland, we each had enough bread and sausage and tubes of squirtable cheese in our backpacks to last about a week.

I remember thinking, This is good, it must mean the war's going to be quick. That's what the high command thought too. But of course it wasn't quick, and we were soon hungry. It is humanly possible to lift shells or march all day on a couple of mess tins' worth of *Wassersuppe*

[literally, water soup, i.e. not thickened with stock or cream].
We did it and so did the Russians. It wasn't long before
some of the partisans were eating grass.

But the hunger, it felt like it was eating us – a furious
spirit trapped inside our bodies like black smoke. And to
appease it we foraged. The farmers, peasants really, destitute
and often barefoot, some of the most elderly ones were
probably the children of serfs, would naturally pretend they
didn't have anything.

We played these grim games of hide and seek with the
old women. The men were all dead or trying to kill us,
the young women in hiding, so the only people left were
groups of mothers and grandmothers, tough *matkas* with
weather-thickened skin, broad cheekbones, missing teeth
and sweat-stained headscarves.

They'd bury big earthenware jars of pickles in their
gardens. We'd take bayonets and crowbars and ram them
into the ground until we hit something. They'd watch in
silence, trying not to react when we got warmer. They'd
wrap an arm round the dirty children holding on to their
legs or peeping out from behind them. When we hit a jar,
they'd look shattered. I suppose they knew what it meant
for them. And if we didn't find anything, we'd start setting
things on fire till they told us.

Even though I was a green young man, a teenager, and
my mother and grandmothers didn't look much like these
women, I was ashamed. But I'd never been in a war before
and I told myself, This is war, this is how wars are fought.
Yesterday I killed half a dozen Ukrainians with a profes-
sionally aimed shell; today I am foraging. This is why

everyone agrees wars are terrible. And taking things from people who don't want to give them up is what war *is*.

But it put an inconspicuous red mark against those days. Later on, when I flicked back through them, I began to see a shameful pattern in the way we were conducting the campaign. I started to realise that we did not hold the high ground. Far from it.

I would never have had to think about this if, through whatever vagaries of paperwork, I'd been assigned to the West. No one planned to starve the populations of Lyon or Bordeaux. But out of simple hunger, rather than malice, we caused very great suffering. And because I was sometimes starving too, I understood what we were doing to these Soviet women and their children when we took their food.

I think about those women sometimes. I go downstairs to the Greek's, where the portions are too big for me, and half the souvlaki with the gravy-soaked *pommes* gets thrown away, and I think of them. It sometimes feels as if they're standing there in some shadow of the restaurant, still watching me from the sidelines. If the postal service could carry things through time and not just space, I'd be able to send them more food than they'd ever seen. And I would.

I don't think I'm a better man now than I was then – more generous, say – nor even really a different man; I was the same man in different times. If I'd been sent West instead of East, if I'd been born in a different year, I'd be innocent of these things. I wasn't in the high command. I didn't make the plans for how the army would be fed. It doesn't seem right to me that I should be blamed. And yet, and yet, while the plan may have been Beck's or Keitel's, or whoever's, it was me who held the crowbar.

Only a very few of us were stronger than our times. Not me. A handful who somehow knew to act beyond themselves, even then, and who have streets named after them now. The rest of us put on the uniforms, dug up the jars of pickles, carried them away and ate them.

It's hard to separate the circumstances from the man. But it isn't as straightforward as saying that I was at the mercy of mine. Just because the times I was living in placed me in those gardens, hungry, with a crowbar in my hand, that doesn't mean I didn't act, or didn't eat.

When I ask myself whether we were all immoral, or whether having done wrong makes us evil men, I think that we were blemished by the consequences of what other people decided. No one ever has complete responsibility for his own moral balance. And the unforgiving truth, the severe, ancient truth, is that you can be culpable for something that you weren't in control of.

And me, personally? That's what I've been trying to answer.

~

Callum: The Greek's he mentions was the in-house restaurant at the luxy old people's residence my grandparents moved into after my opa retired. His apartment there must be where he wrote this letter. It's less like a care home than a spa hotel in the off season, with a pool and balconies where we'd sit and talk after dinner.

Because their apartment was on the eighth floor, and the building is on a hill above a plain, if you sit there your eyesight reaches its own limit before it finds the horizon. You can see tiny planes silently touching down at an American military airport, on their way to or from Afghanistan and Iraq; also the blunt grey boxes of factories and plants, medium-sized manufacturers, famous among economists as the source of Germany's affluence; you can see the occasional glint of a silver filament threaded through the plain – that's the Rhine; and in the far distance you can see the big red sun sinking over France.

View aside, I never liked it much. My grandparents moved there prematurely from their previous house, which I loved. With typical prudence, they decided that they didn't want the last phase of their lives to be a dreary wait for the big sleep, and moved while they were still young enough to enjoy the old people's home. My granddad must have been in his late sixties. My oma, early sixties I suppose. It was by far the fanciest thing they'd ever done. I think my granddad thought the expense was worth it because my oma would be happy there.

They switched from a slow, restful village life to some-thing almost like an American summer camp. Suddenly it was all activities and socialising, in the heavily routinised way the retirees liked. Mondays: pottery. Tuesdays: walking group, followed by *Kaffee und Kuchen* with Frau von Hasselbach. Wednesdays: wine circle. Thursdays: more pottery. Fridays: bowling at the traditional German nine-pin bowling alley. As a visiting teenager, I'd go along with my grandparents and whup the oldsters. Not having arthritis gives you an edge. Some of the old guys were still competitive enough for it to piss them off.

My oma picked up a year-long fixation on pottery and started churning out ashtrays in the shapes of leaves. Six or seven a week, because she was so productive. Even though she didn't smoke. I don't think she knew anyone who smoked. But ashtrays were the instructor's speciality, so that's what she threw herself into. She'd be there in the craft room two afternoons a week, wearing a smudgy potter's apron over her cardigans and beige skirts, so engrossed that she barely noticed the other ladies. Most of them came to chat and eat biscuits; my oma came to work. She was competitive, too, smiling to herself on the way back upstairs if she felt she'd really blown Frau Whoever's offering out of the water.

Next to the in-house restaurant was a display window where the produce from the various craft groups was put on sale for good causes. Most people from the groups contributed a knitted scarf, a set of clay wind chimes, something like that. With my oma, while the craze lasted, it was more like sixty-two ashtrays, eight pairs of knitted socks, three jumpers and four patterned scarves, all of wool so scratchy I couldn't bear to put them on. I've still got a pair that I can only wear when it's cold enough to have some normal socks on underneath.

I think they felt that, as the new people, they had to make an effort. And as they said constantly for the first couple of years, they'd never had anything like this back in the village.

The Greek's was one of the attractions, where we'd go

for birthdays or the first day of a visit. The food was pretty lazily put together, basically kebabs on plates. The point of going wasn't that it was good, but that the trellised vines and decorative amphorae made it obvious that we were celebrating. I don't mean that my opa had any lack of warmth, but his manner was contained, orderly, finding it easier to show affection through bookings and organised treats than through spontaneity of expression. My oma had done most of the child-rearing; after she died, he was worried that if he didn't lay on the right things, perhaps we wouldn't be sure we'd celebrated at all.

Aside from special occasions, at the Greek's, say, or a properly sumptuous hotel restaurant in town – a venison-steak, silver-cutlery-and-bowing-waiters kind of a place – he and my oma ate the same meal every evening for as long as I knew them: dense black bread, butter, pre-sliced cheese and ham. There were also thick soft discs of *Gelbwurst*, a type of sausage I liked as a child and which he therefore bought in bulk every time I visited. On some evenings he would hard-boil two eggs, to be sliced onto the bread, and on the last night of my visit he might divide a bottle of beer equally into two glasses. I never knew him to express any interest in eating anything else, nor in eating what he did.

I don't think it was wartime hunger that defined his relationship with food. It was more that he would have found the idea of a 'relationship with food' to be fatuous. Where you did see the war's mark was with waste or excess. After slicing bread, he'd sweep up the crumbs with the edge of his hand and pour them back into the paper bag. At the

Greek's, where even a 'senior's portion' was too big, he'd eat past the point of pain unless we intervened to split the extra meat and chips between us.

If trying to describe what kind of man he was when I knew him, those traits jump out: the austerity of his habits, both of body and mind; his uninterest in self-indulgence; and yet the way he would indulge almost anything he thought would make someone happy. If I didn't want to finish my plate, he let it go, because it was me. I picture his moral sense as a grid of perfectly straight lines that covers the whole world and all possible situations. But wherever the lines reached someone he loved, they spiralled into a little twist of affection and loyalty, like a knot in wood.

He'd wanted to be a chemical scientist, but when the war squashed that, he ended up running a pharmacy in a village an hour from Heidelberg. Thwarted ambition or no, he built it up with that unrelenting German pragmatism. By small business standards, he made a heap of cash. He shelved it carefully in bonds, land, gold, things that couldn't catch fire or blow up. Then, as the business kept bringing in more, he put it in secondary insurance policies, emergency funds, holdings of last resort; accounts in his children's names in case he was ever in trouble; a dollar account in Switzerland in case the German banking system was ever in trouble, which I suppose he had actually seen before. On and on he went until retirement, building fail-safes for every threat he could imagine, rings of walls and moats and crenellations and towers between the family and the wolf at the door.

But he shelled out gratefully so that my oma could make ashtrays and they could visit their innumerable neighbours for *Kaffee und Kuchen* afterwards. That was the measure of his happiness. A small life, perhaps. A quiet one, certainly. Too quiet for me. When I visited, he'd inflict proud-granddad stories on his wine circle about how I'd just been filming a (very formulaic) travel show in Spain or how busy my life was in London – even though he would have hated doing either of those himself.

He was a minister's son and there's a stereotype, I'm sure often deserved, about Protestants: a certain severity, meanness and distrust of joy. But I was as marinated in adoration as any favoured grandchild could have ever been. In the German board games we played on the balcony table, *Stratego* and *Barrikade*, I cheated continuously and was never questioned. My grandparents' freely given love was so cosy that I simply assumed I'd been born with remarkable sleight of hand. Until I was an adult, it literally didn't occur to me that they'd known all along.

So, as to the question of his goodness or otherwise as a man, you know the caveat: I'm his grandson and I loved him. And yet he fought for the Nazis. Wore the uniform, killed people. Did the things he talks about here. I loved him so much I ask myself whether I would have forgiven him anything. Probably not *anything*, though it makes me sad just to say that.

~

Only a few minutes from where we'd been dug in, our little fanned-out search party walked into the deep quiet of empty countryside. One of the strangest aspects of the war was how close you could be to it without any sign it was going on. It wasn't like it had been for our fathers' generation, with those parallel trenches slithering across Europe. Some Germans were in these woods or on those hills, some Russians in this collective farm or that swamp – we were always looking for each other, getting off some blows and then running away again.

On the map, there hadn't been much in the way of landmarks: a small village and a nearby manor house, both of which we presumed had already been looted. Other than that, the area was like everything I saw of Poland: wide, flat farmland; stands of gloomy forest; and a full day's march from one wretched wooden hamlet to the next.

When we arrived there in the invasion – before the army, I'd never been out of Lower Saxony, a place of broom-swept streets and gardening contests – I was amazed by how miserable, how destitute, it was. I kept thinking of the phrase *polnische Wirtschaft* [Polish housekeeping, i.e. slovenly and backward], which you don't hear now, naturally, but was then a normal way of describing things. And I thought, Why have we started a war for – well, what other word is there for it – for this shithole? These people don't have anything.

The Russians, for their part, the Kazakhs and Chechens, must have been incensed when they arrived in Germany and saw how well we lived; that we who were rich had come to rob them who were poor. I'm sure that's part of why they behaved the way they did when they first got their hands on our families and neighbours. That twists the heart, to think about it. But of course, of course, we'd already done so much worse to them.

In the East, only the countryside was beautiful. I remember one autumn dawn when the mist was so thick it looked as if the herds of cattle were swimming in it, just their heads and backs breaking the surface. And one night, when we were driving in moonlight, there was so much mist swirling in the fields it looked like silvery water, with the trees mirrored in it by their shadows. So much beauty, especially for a town-born boy like me.

So I was glad to be away from the firing positions and out under the shifting sky. Autumn was the most humane season and, if I walked at a distance from the others, I couldn't really hear their conversation. In the army there is always someone talking. Lüttke was boasting about his father-in-law's fancy car, which he apparently paid a boy from the neighbourhood to polish every Sunday. That is the sort of nonsense you hear for years on end.

In the open meadows we went through, there were patches where the knee-high grass had burned away and the exposed earth underneath was toasted black. The grass was mixed with taller stalks of some kind of wheat, which swayed and murmured around us when the air moved. I picked the ripe ears out of it and chewed as we went along.

We kept tripping over smashed military litter: broken rifles, shreds of cartridge paper, dented mess bowls, water canisters, ammunition boxes, belts, milk tins. The litter of battle. I saw a typewriter with blades of grass sliding up through the keys, and near it an abandoned wooden plough, with a rank patch of bones and hide still under the yoke. Most of this stuff was Soviet. The belt buckles showed a crudely cast hammer and sickle in the centre of a spindly star. Ours said *Gott Mit Uns*. Our fathers, including mine, who was a chaplain in the first war, had had that etched into their helmets, for all the good it did anyone.

We were so low on brass for shell casings that we were sometimes told to scavenge through this sort of detritus for spent cartridges to be sent back to Germany. I doubt many ever got there. The shells we got were so stingily made they exploded in the barrel, blowing out a steel bubble halfway along its length, like an arthritic knuckle.

We kicked and prodded this jetsam to see if it held anything edible, but it had lain there long enough to be grown over by weeds and nettles. By the next year, the burned patches in the fields would have been filled in. The signs of war were being covered over. The country was healing as we were pushed out of it.

Nevertheless, as I walked along, the stress and fear of being in the forward positions began to seep out of me. It had been very bad recently. If I'd shared my father's belief in what would happen after I was killed – eternal bliss – perhaps I would have had more equanimity about it. As it was I was driven through every day by a powerful desire not to die. It held the need to sleep at arm's length. But while I stumbled through those scorched meadows, fatigue started grabbing at my legs. I was so tired it hurt. One of the Russians' tactics was to break us down psychologically by keeping us awake: they'd let off flurries of yowling Katyusha rockets at irregular intervals, and I would have a recurring nightmare that a pack of dogs was chasing me all the way from Moscow to home. They must have kept themselves awake as well, but everything's easier to bear when you're winning.

My steps were gradually losing their momentum. I found myself squinting up at the mid-morning sky, entering that blissful state just before sleep when you've already surrendered and all you need to do is fall. The sky seemed to become mysterious and benevolent, as if it were watching me.

My body began dreaming of how soft the earth would be. My head rolled on my neck . . . But it didn't happen. One of the others – Ottermann, the big, clever, straw-blond Frisian farmer with the Viking's beard – shouted to us all to come over. We trudged into a weary huddle. I dropped to the ground, not taking off my helmet, and closed my eyes. I would have been out cold if Ottermann hadn't nudged me in the ribs with his boot.

He pointed at me and said, This one's passed out on his feet.

I was too exhausted to mind the attention, so I just nodded. Ottermann wanted us to lie down in the grass and sleep for a few hours before we did anything else. It was the certainty of sleep now versus the possibility of finding food later; I didn't even try to have an opinion. Lüttke wanted us to push on. Not, I think, because he thought the food stores were nearby, but because he assumed that pushing on was the right attitude for a promotion candidate. To my dulled astonishment, he said something about the 'iron will of the German soldier'. I opened my eyes a little to check whether he was joking, but he didn't seem to be.

The phrase was a propaganda slogan, of the sort that had become running gags. There was one – 'For all this we thank the Führer' – that had been plastered across pictures of new autobahns and factories in the Thirties. Now, whenever you saw the crashed fuselage of one of our planes, or a field so thickly strewn with our dead that it was like a whole herd had been struck by lightning, someone would say, 'For all this . . .'

Through the crack under my eyelids, I saw Lüttke was being serious. And, despite the cloak, he didn't look like he was giving up his hold on reality – something you had to watch for.

Ottermann asked him, What's the matter with you? Are you crazy or something?

Lüttke was offended. He said, Is it crazy to think German soldiers shouldn't just lie down in a field like a bunch of lazy-arsed Bolsheviks? Or would you prefer it if we *were* all Bolsheviks, Ottermann?

The others told Lüttke they had no interest in displaying an iron will. If he didn't want to sleep, that was his business. But someone pointed out that the hamlet we'd seen on the map might be only a bit further on. We didn't have a map of our own – only officers had maps – but from what people could remember, it might be just beyond the stand of trees at the edge of this meadow. The Poles would presumably have some food as well as somewhere to sleep.

Lüttke seized on the idea, and said, We could search the place for partisans while we're there.

Exclamations of anger and outrage burst from the others. We were all rightly afraid of the partisans.

Ottermann said, The important thing is, the important thing is . . .

He paused until the others paid attention, then said to Lüttke, The important thing is, if you're that crazy, maybe you shouldn't be trusted with the pony.

I opened my eyes again to watch. He reached out a big hand, like a shovel blade, towards Ferdinand's rope, but stopped it in mid-air, cocked, as if asking a question. He made it look nonchalant, but I think it ate him up that Ferdinand belonged to someone who knew so much less about horses than he did.

Lüttke, predictably enough, took it badly. The possibility that the rest of us might agree made him shiver with aggression. He slapped Ottermann's hand away and said, You can come lick my arse, you Lenin-loving pig [German swearing takes its metaphors from the farmyard]. Get a job and buy your own shitting pony.

Ottermann pulled on one of the plaits at the end of his beard and seemed to be assessing how hard it would be to throw Lüttke on the ground. I'm sure he could have. The other two were still hung up on the mention of partisans and started warily swapping horror stories, most of which I'd heard before.

The more everyone talked, the more talking felt to me like a needless irritation. The wave of sleep had broken before it could engulf me, and retreated. I rubbed my face and climbed to my feet. I generally preferred not to speak up in the army, because it eroded the barrier between my private self and the army's collective mind. But while this indecisive conversation went on, our tiredness and hunger were steadily sharpening. I said, Since we're not getting any closer to sleep, we might as well get closer to the food. So let's get on with it.

Ottermann said, Are you sure you wouldn't rather have another lie down?

I didn't enjoy this kind of ribbing, so I just said, I'm fine.

Ottermann shrugged his heavy frame and said, Fine by me. Off we go then.

No one disagreed and we started trudging again. This time we didn't bother to fan out. I was walking slightly in front, but I didn't want it to seem that I was leading. I slowed down and, as I let myself be overtaken, Lüttke dropped an arm around my shoulders.

He was a bit shorter, so it felt like he was trying to drag me down into a headlock as we walked along. I kept having to dodge his breath as he turned to speak at me. To be fair, mine probably stank as badly as his. We hadn't had tooth-paste for a while.

He told me confidentially, It's a shame we haven't had a chance to talk before this. I can see you're a real old stalwart in the making, aren't you? I can see that, I know all there is to know about being a judge of character, believe me. I've seen a lot of guys meet their moment of truth, a lot. You're a young guy but with that proper Stalingrad spirit. How long have you been in the war?

I didn't answer the question, just told him I came in as a gunner.

And he went on, I never considered anything except infantry myself – I prefer to fight on my two feet, man to man, but the artillery's a good thing. Bet you wish we still had those guns now, don't you?

He laughed and squeezed my neck, then said, But don't worry: these shitty Russians won't get past us. And it's proper technical work, isn't it, being in the artillery. You've got to have a head for figures, like I do, too. I worked in a bank, back in Berlin. But I didn't want to do that when I joined up. I wanted to be out there on the front line, giving it to them right in the face. Not miles behind the line shooting at something in the distance. But that technical work's important, too. Like being a sapper. Probably not what people back home think of when they imagine their brave boys fighting the Bolsheviks, but still, vital work, yes, vital. How long have you been in the war? I've been in for two and a bit years myself. Got my *Obergefreiter*, can't imagine it'll be long before they give me *Unteroffizier*. And you?

I said I'd been in since Barbarossa, and it made him unsure of himself. Abruptly he became more swaggering, more disdainful, apparently the way he imagined a big man to be. But he was right: there was something unsettling about having survived so long. In that time, entire new armies had been raised and trained and marched out fresh from home, bands playing and pennants fluttering; they'd passed in front of me and, like the children of Hamelin, marched on into the earth. I'd stayed above it.

It doesn't show me in a kind light to say it, but some-times, especially when dozens and hundreds of people are being killed at once, it's exhilarating to survive. When bits of metal were fizzing around me as thick as rain, with great lumps of shells looping here and there over my head to explode around me, and not one of them so much as crinkled my uniform – then it felt like the dreams children have about being born imbued with hidden magic, that I was impervious to harm, and my ordinary exterior concealed someone different from the rest.

But once that battle euphoria had worn off, my hands would shake so hard I couldn't hold a spoon. I'd be convinced that each bullet that missed had shortened the odds for the next one, making it certain I'd be hit tomorrow. Objectively, it was just a question of probabilities. Three million of us went East in Barbarossa; some of us lived all the way through. It's just that our minds are still too close to the caveman's to really understand randomness.

In any case, when Lüttke heard it, he told me, not very believably, that he'd volunteered right at the beginning, in 1939. But that because he worked in a bank he was too vital to fight right away. If he'd been in as long as I had, he had no doubt he'd be a senior *Unteroffizier* by now.

I wanted to shrug him off, so that the others, and him for that matter, didn't think that I was somehow on his side. But it would have just meant having to talk to him even more in the ensuing argument.

So we carried on with him deploring that they were handing out Iron Crosses like cigarettes these days. You could get the cross and oak leaves just for what he'd always considered his everyday duty. He himself had been offered the Iron Cross, but his captain was killed before he could submit the recommendation. He wouldn't have wanted it anyway, because they were so cheap nowadays. All this with his hot breath tickling my ear.

We reached the stand of pine trees we thought separated us from the village. Some of the trunks had been pocked by bullets. The holes had had time to stretch and deform, so they probably pre-dated the military litter in the meadow. Among the trees we found a collapsed Soviet jeep, one of the junky Russian models they'd depended on before they started getting American replacements. It was rusted down and entangled up to its wheel arches in ferns and under-growth. In and near it were a few leathery corpses in Russian uniforms, who'd been shrivelling long enough for the cloth to be slack across what was left inside. They were probably from when we'd come through here the first time, heading East.

They had nothing useful on them, and I'm sure I'd never have remembered them if what happened afterwards hadn't snipped these days out of memory's reel. We soon left them and pushed through the thick undergrowth to the other side of the woods. The village wasn't there. Nor was the miraculous food store.

I think defeat was harder for us than for other nations, and in the end it broke us more completely. The Romanians, from what I could see, were already used to thinking of themselves as downtrodden. For them, being in the army must have been a nearly feudal experience. Their officers wore those black cloaks and hit them with riding crops. They were pre-modern: barely trained, shoddily equipped and led by dilettantes. To them, there was no difference between morale and discipline. Capitulation can't have bothered them much.

From what I saw, it was similar for the other allies – the Italians, Hungarians, Croats and so on, the other Balkan countries. I never met any Finns, but my impression is that they were engaged in their own private business with Russia and didn't care about the rest of the war. The others seemed to have less pride invested in it than we did. Or, at least, for the Italians, their pride was flexible enough to allow switching to the winning side.

We Germans have always been touchier. And we'd gone from being the new masters of Europe to being the hated Germans, the fucking Germans, what the Russians called 'the accursed Germany'. And being hated while you're winning is one thing; it's quite another to be hated while you lose.

We knew that retribution was coming, and what it looked like. In the East, I'd seen so many corpses – thousands, maybe tens of thousands – and I'd seen the corpses of everything. Young women, babies, old people stripped naked by a blast. Limbs thrown into branches and dangling from telephone lines. Cows, horses, pigs, dogs. Dead tanks, dead cars, dead trains, ships crashed into riverbanks and planes shot down into fields. Houses shattered, towns emptied. I'd seen whole cities standing in flame. That was what we'd done to the East. And now the Russians – the Russians were coming for us, vengeful and numberless. Even in 1942 they'd sometimes outnumbered us seven or eight to one.

They'd always been as brave as us – a wasteful, shocking kind of bravery, heedless of themselves. Even at the beginning, when they were on the chopping block, they'd die to protect a tank that we were going to blow up anyway or to hold some burning village for an extra five minutes. They'd charge at machine guns, eight ranks deep. We didn't do that. We'd see them running into the pitiless chatter of our MG42s in their long leather cloaks, shaven-headed young men shouting, *Urrah! Urrah!* It makes the hair on my forearms stand on end to think of it.

And once they'd recovered from the shock of invasion, they started to learn about soldiering. At the beginning, I suppose because Stalin had sent all the good officers to the Gulag, they had no idea what to do. Instead of massing their tanks, they'd split them up and park each one alone, perfectly silhouetted on the crest of a ridge. For us in the artillery, it was like being back on the firing range.

But the ones who'd lived had learned. While we were getting worse at being an army, they were getting better. It had reached the humbling point at which they were using their huge advantage in numbers and materiel not just to over-roll, but to outmanoeuvre us. Pincers, cauldrons, combined-arms assaults, attempts to 'defeat in detail': we could see them learning the textbook on us.

As the possibility that we were going to lose thickened into certainty, we began to count up the terrible things we'd done. We were rightly afraid of what the Russians would do to us in return. Our sisters and mothers raped by soldiers. Our businesses and factories dismantled and shipped off. Those of us in uniform enslaved and sent to the mines in Siberia. All of which happened. Lots of men, when they finally came home, preferred not to know too much about how their families had passed the years while they were away.

There was a joke that was now always trotted out whenever someone complained: 'Enjoy the war, the peace will be much worse.' It always made me think of my school Latin, and the story about Rome being sacked by Brennus the Gaul. The Romans had agreed to pay Brennus to leave the city. When they were weighing out the stipulated price in gold and silver, they complained that the scales were rigged against them. Brennus threw his sword on top, making it worse, and said, *Vae victis*, woe to the conquered. That's what it means to be at someone's mercy.

The mood of the propaganda shifted accordingly. Since Stalingrad, it had been full of stories about unexpected changes of fortune. They said there might be another Russian Revolution, as in our fathers' time. Or there was the 'miracle of Brandenburg' in the Seven Years' War, when the Russian troops advancing on Berlin stopped because the tsarina had died of a stroke. The message was that there might be another miracle. We should fight on and give it the chance to occur.

The landings in Normandy finished off any sane hope, despite all the talk about throwing the Americans back into the sea. Now the propaganda kept hinting at glorious death against overwhelming odds. Last stands. That bloated fantasist Goering was always talking on the radio about the Spartans dying at Thermopylae to delay the Eastern horde. Their self-sacrifice had supposedly saved Europe from being overrun by the Asiatics. I remember him saying that the Spartans' epitaph was carved into the rubble at Stalingrad:

TRAVELLER, IF YOU GO TO SPARTA,
TELL THEM YOU SAW US LYING HERE,
AS THE LAW COMMANDED.

Dying as the law commanded was plainly the suggestion. The idea didn't make me feel noble and glorious, no matter how much they wrapped it up. Especially as I didn't imagine that Reichsmarschall Goering and his friends would be laying down their own lives, only ours.

There were suicides, more and more of them. Someone would go off to fetch water or rations and not come back. No one wanted to go looking, because you might find them slumped with their rifle in their lap. Also, if their deaths were reported as suicides, their families wouldn't get a military pension. So we preferred not to look, and to assume that the Russians or the partisans had got them.

It was almost always under the trees. In the way that animals crawl under something when it's time to die, very few could bear to shoot themselves under the open sky.

But sometimes whole groups would shoot themselves together. Usually it would build up around a couple of men who'd served together for a long time, or even known each other before the war. I suppose each reminded the other that he had once been a man, not just a louse trying to evade the pinching fingers.

The group would go into the woods, drink bottles of stolen cognac, get sentimental, raise toasts until the cognac was finished and then all shoot themselves at once. There's a melancholy in us Germans at the best of times, a weakness for sad songs and long goodbyes. I'm sure they wished the cognac would last for ever.

I saw these group suicides several times and never thought they were brave or honourable. The dead looked ridiculous, lolling like drunken picnickers with their brains on the ground beside them. It made me ashamed of our famous European civilisation, that it had no more than this to offer, in mental resources, in philosophical consolation, to the people born into it.

I felt better about what was called a soldier's death: someone would climb out of his hole and walk slowly towards the Russians, firing his rifle. Unless there happened to be one of their beloved snipers about, it could take a long time before they hit him. He'd keep walking and reloading until finally someone managed to knock him over.

Now it just seems sad and absurd, but back then it had a certain primitive dignity. I don't deny that it appealed to me from time to time. I daydreamed about it as a moment of manumission, light-hearted and solemn: you got up off your knees; the ignominies of exhaustion and fear would drop away; you'd free yourself from duty, obligation and the necessity of survival, simply by standing up.

Sitting at my quiet table in an orderly suburb, it seems a barbaric distinction to make. The electric buses go up and down the hill, schoolchildren with colourful backpacks tumble along the street in the afternoons, and it seems incredible to be so old that I've lived in both that time and this. These days, a good end is a short illness.

The reason I didn't act on that daydream was ultimately that, out of whatever perseverance or naivety, I never quite ceased to believe that good decisions could help me. Those who chose to die had abdicated from the chore of thought; they capitulated to the despair that said none of it would make any difference.

I'm very grateful now that I didn't. I had forty-six years with your oma. Fewer than I wanted, yes, fewer than I planned for. But many more than I could have claimed to merit.

Some people, with an impulse typical of the era, took what was really a simple way to end your life and orchestrated it to the heights of grandiosity. Günther Lütjens, for one – you won't have heard of him, but everyone my age knows his name. He was an admiral on the flagship *Bismarck*, a huge thing, a floating fortress. The British somehow managed to hit it in the rudder. A lucky shot, right in the Achilles heel, which meant that this vast fighting machine could only steam in circles. It was alone and the British fleet was still nearby, tracking the wounded giant. Even if Lütjens hadn't cared about saving his crew, even if he'd just wanted to win the war at any cost, the rational decision would have been to fire a few more barrages and then surrender. Perhaps one day all those highly trained sailors might escape captivity.

Instead he opened the ship's stores so everyone could eat and drink as much as they wanted, and declared that they'd fight to the last drop of blood. The English gunners duly bludgeoned the *Bismarck* into a shapeless piece of steel, as they had to, and Lütjens went down with his ship. The

Nazis loved it, and something like two thousand men died in the sea.

I saw the same attraction to spectacle in the army. Small groups would arrange a private *Götterdämmerung* for themselves. They'd steal some *panzerfausts* – hand-held rockets that weren't big enough to get through the Russians' armour – and go off to attack a full-strength Soviet tank battalion. The plan was always the same: go down in an apocalypse of shellfire, the rows of tank barrels blaring like the trumpets at the end of the world. They'd lay out their blaze of glory like any other operation – where they'd hide, where they'd open fire and where the Russians would kill them all.

I wouldn't be surprised if many of them really were thinking of the Spartans, or the *Nibelungenlied*. It wasn't just propaganda. Or rather, the reason the propaganda worked, and why that whole period is so painful to think about now, is that it spoke to something that did exist in many of us. All this hoo-ha and pathos about the Spartans and the Nibelungs did touch something real.

There was more than a whiff of silliness to these grand tragedies, these pantomimes of valour, with the Russians pushed into a role as the agents of fate. But still I preferred them to the suicides. And I preferred them to what I saw many people around me do, which was just stop trying. They dug their holes sloppily, they went for cover at a jog, and finally someone shot them.

Looking back on it now, I can't quite reason out how it was better to go down firing at some Russian teenagers, maybe killing them, rather than just lying down quietly and waiting to be finished off. I suppose that would have been the moral choice, the one of least harm. But still, there's something in us that capitulation offends.

~

Callum: Because it's barely known in English, I should say that the *Nibelungenlied* is one of the set texts of German culture, like a gloomy northern *Iliad*, except not as good. Show me someone who's read the whole thing and I'll show you someone with an exam coming up. With a side-by-side modern translation and an undergrad module on historical linguistics, I'm one of the handful of people in Britain who've actually read it, which means I can slag it off from inside the tent.

The story is about knights killing each other in a series of murky vendettas. Ultimately, the Nibelungs, a band of doomed Germanic warriors, are surrounded in their castle by an Eastern multitude, in this case the Huns. The Nibelungs refuse to surrender despite the hopeless odds. The Huns set the place alight and the 'song of the Nibelungs' relates how our heroes die unyielding in the fire.

It's where Wagner got the material for the Ride of the Valkyries and the *Götterdämmerung*, the twilight of the gods. The Nibelungs are the expression of a Scandi-Germanic world view in which, at the end of time, the gods fight a battle against the forces of chaos and unreason – and lose. The gods are defeated, but don't consider that defeat a refutation.

Rather than ending with paradise on earth, the world

goes back to what it was at the beginning: blind matter, hostile and meaningless. Since there's no eternal bliss to get to, the highest virtue isn't goodness but courage. The best of men get to fight alongside the gods in the final battle and share their defiance, more perfect because it is without hope.

I should say that this end-of-days fixation is only one very narrow, atavistic niche in German culture, brought out by the extreme despair of losing two world wars. These are the same people who are really committed to recycling.

~

When we went through that little stand of trees, and the village we'd been expecting wasn't there, we almost gave up the whole expedition. My life would have turned out differently. But since we were already on our feet, we kept walking. We hiked across another meadow, went over a small hill, through some more trees, and there, finally, were the village's remnants. It looked like a graveyard in a fever dream: a couple of dozen misshapen columns of brick with beds of ash in front of them – the stoves and chimney stacks of burned-out wooden houses. When we saw them, we dropped to the scrubby ground, seeking the earth with our hands, and crawled into cover.

All I could see among the ash were the charred stumps of roof timbers. Almost nothing these people owned would withstand a fire. Some metal pots, perhaps. Things we would have put in a bag they wrapped in cabbage leaves.

It looked recent. The grass hadn't yet drawn its green

blur over the destruction, and the ash hadn't been dissolved by rain. If we'd kicked through the wreckage, we might still have found some warmth in the soil. Perhaps we Germans had done this to punish the people who'd lived here for helping the partisans. Perhaps the partisans had done it to punish them for helping us. Perhaps it had just happened, in the way things did in war.

Ottermann, the big Frisian, just said, Partisans round here.

He was talking to one of the others, Jansen, a younger, frightened man who he looked after a bit. He hadn't been at the front at all long, and was so fresh that he still had the boyish colour in his cheeks. He and Ottermann were from the same part of the country. Jansen wasn't from Frisia, exactly, but from not far away, in Hamburg. I think he'd been a dockworker, from a family of dockworkers. He must have been called up when the docks were destroyed. Ottermann was trying to show him what to look for.

That was Jansen's best chance, to watch and imitate those, like Ottermann, who'd reached the point of expertise at which whatever killed them was unlikely to be their fault. But Jansen seemed not to want to adapt. He wasn't developing the cautious, ruthless, practical outer layer, alert to threat but numb to trauma, that characterised the people who survived longest. To be fair to him, if I'd arrived in the war at this late stage I might not have seen much worth in imitating the people who'd got us to where we were.

So Jansen complained, he talked, he let his skin stay thin. Perhaps he thought that there was so little of the war left, he could somehow keep it from going into him. It made me think he wasn't going to last long. And indeed he didn't.

He said to Ottermann, Do you think this thing about the food was a trick to get us out here?

Ottermann pushed the end of one of his beard plaits into his mouth and bit into it. Then he spat it out again and said, I don't know. I don't think so.

Do you think maybe we should just go back? We're not supposed to be round here anyway, are we? If the partisans want this place, they can have it, in my opinion.

I ran my eye across the brick totems, searching methodically for something unexpected. I wasn't sleepy any more. As we watched, the sun turned itself up, brightening the ground and drawing shadows across the beds of ash. It seemed pretty unlikely to me that any partisans would be hiding behind the bricks. But they could be among the trees at the edge of the village.

Lüttke turned on Jansen, saying, Shut your mouth, Jansen. This shithole belongs to us, partisans or no partisans. If you want to give up, why don't you just go shoot yourself now and save us the whining.

Ferdinand the pony was pulling at his rope, unperturbed by what we were up to, and trying to get closer to some tasty-looking flowers. Ottermann and I glanced at each other and nodded. Ottermann said, We should do leapfrogs.

I said, Yep.

Me and Jansen will go first.

Alright.

Lüttke said, We should do a flanking manoeuvre. Two groups. Ottermann, you take your little friend and

Himmelsbach. I'll take Meissner. I'll give you the signal when it's—

Ottermann simply ignored him. While Lüttke talked, he cajoled the reluctant Jansen into a crouch, and then the two of them sprinted forward to belly-flop down again on the open ground a dozen metres ahead of us. Lüttke, like the rest of us, had no choice. He tied Ferdinand's rope to a branch, swearing under his breath, and followed.

We went through our small unit tactics, those in front providing cover while those behind rushed past them. An overlapping relay of short, angled sprints. These days I see it when I'm watching football on television, and the strikers make diagonal bursts into the penalty box.

My pack banged up and down on my back, and I was soon panting, but no one shot at us. There was no sound but what little we were making. I began to relax again. We got in among the ash and the chimney stacks, and when it was my turn I ran forward and hid behind one of the columns, not leaning on it in case it toppled over.

Up close, I caught the stale complex smell of a burned-out fire. In the ash I noticed a pair of spoons still nestled into each other, warped but perfectly usable. I stretched across to pick them out, wiped them on my blue trousers and dropped them into my tunic pocket. It occurred to me that this village would have gardens, most likely with potatoes still in the ground.

Jansen sprinted past me and into cover behind the next stack. But instead of kneeling down, he stood upright, unslung his rifle and threw it down at his feet. He turned around and walked back towards us.

53

Ottermann hissed at him, Get down, Jansen! Get down! What the hell are you doing?

But Jansen was furious. He pulled off his helmet and threw that on the ground as well. Then started fumbling at his tunic. When he got closer, I could see that he was crying through his anger.

I realise that I started by saying I wasn't going to tell you about atrocities. But these things have a gravity of their own. They bend your lines of thought towards them. Now here we are.

To put it bluntly: hanging from a single big tree were all the villagers, in bunches, like swollen plums. They were rotting where they dangled. All different ages. A flock of glutted crows was crowded onto their shoulders and heads, and the thick branches were bending with the weight.

To my shame, I'd seen people hanged before – civilians, lots of them, and some people I'd sat next to at meals – but never anything like this. The tree was full to the upper branches. A few had been shot in the legs or belly, perhaps when they'd tried to grab on to each other.

No one spoke. Eventually Lüttke said, Partisans, and Ottermann walked away so as not to hit him. The rest of us just kept looking. I saw Himmelsbach, the fifth person in our group and the only south German, cross himself.

The crows had pecked holes into their faces, which were black or bright yellow. Eyeless, lipless, with teeth visible through rips in the cheeks. Some heads had come off, like stoppers, and the bodies dropped to the ground below. Animals, maybe foxes or the village dogs, had chewed through their clothes and pulled out their ribs.

I'm sorry to say it never occurred to me to cut them down, or do anything for them at all. I doubt it did to anyone else either. Even our own dead we didn't bury any more.

It would have been different if we'd found them three years earlier. Back then, in summer and autumn of 1941, there was still a certain ceremony to death. We'd inter our dead in a neat line, often in the graveyard of a village we'd just seized. Sometimes there'd already be a row of squint weather-corroded crosses from the last time Germans were there, in 1916.

We'd walk the line of graves with a kind of childish seriousness and leave wildflowers on the older ones. Some-one with a Leica would take pictures to send to the families, along with directions: your husband is buried two days' march East of Bialystok, in a village spelled something like . . . But after a while, well, I suppose there were just too many.

Now I wish I'd done something for those people. But perhaps it's just that, with hindsight, I've adopted the perspective of someone who wasn't there. People always imagine that, in these situations, *their* humanity would have shone through.

And burying them might have just been selfishness anyway – a small decision that disguised our bigger one to continue participating in the war. But the truth is probably that it doesn't matter a jot how we felt about it: we should have done something for them, and we didn't.

What we actually did do was start shouting at each other. The argument was nominally about whether this was the same village we'd seen on the captain's map. I remember yelling the first thing that came into my head, about how this wasn't even where we were supposed to be, we should have stayed in the sector we'd been given – and what was the use of doing anything if we weren't going to follow the plan.

Jansen was still trying to pull off his tunic and practically shrieking that we had to get away; the food was a partisan trick; they were going to hang us as well. Himmelsbach, the south German, was swearing about what the shit were these people even still doing here with the shitting Russians just down the road. Lüttke was shoving Jansen and telling him to pick up his rifle.

As we stood there yelling at each other amid the surrounding quiet of the countryside, Ottermann came back over to us with something he'd found. He wordlessly held up two empty bottles of champagne, real French Bollinger with bright foil on the necks, torn from when the corks were popped.

We stopped shouting. No one in Poland was drinking Bollinger but us. Ottermann passed us the bottles and went to retrieve Jansen's rifle. I remember weighing one in my hand and feeling the heavy thickness of the base.

Ottermann came back with Jansen's rifle and made him hold it. He re-fastened the buttons on Jansen's tunic and put his helmet back on him. Then he led us over to where he'd found the bottles. Pressed into the packed earth of what had been the village square was a trail of caterpillar tracks, which arrived, turned around and went back the way they'd come. The earth was crumbly, but the marks were quite fresh and perfectly clear: narrow with a smooth line running down the middle. They belonged to a model of half-track we had, a trailer pulled by a motorbike. Unmistakably ours.

Strewn around were a few more champagne bottles, and only champagne, as if our brothers-in-arms wouldn't drink anything less. Also the butts from real cigarettes and shiny brass cartridge casings, some squashed where the caterpillar tracks had gone over them. Without needing to confer, Lüttke went back to collect Ferdinand. While he was gone, we stood there and thought our thoughts.

Horses are more sensitive to the human world than many other animals. Corpses spook them. When Lüttke brought Ferdinand, the poor pony pressed his ears back and lowered his head, cringing. Lüttke yanked him forward and Ottermann said, Don't do that again if you don't want a kicking. That horse has more sense than you do.

Lüttke didn't respond, but when Ottermann turned away, I saw the tip of Lüttke's rifle twitch and drift for a moment towards Ottermann's back. We were all overwrought.

We set off along the tracks, close together, our weapons lifted. The ground was soft and, even though the motorised trailers were nowhere near as heavy as tanks, the tracks were easy to follow. They led past some more of the burned-out brick columns and then into some woods, with pine trees on either side and shadows beneath them.

After a while, we came across another champagne bottle, tossed on the verge. When Jansen noticed, he charged over to it. I thought he was going to pick it up, but he turned round and shouted at the rest of us, How much shitting champagne can they even drink?

Ottermann told him to keep walking. Jansen didn't budge. He just stared at us, getting wilder rather than calmer. Then he lifted his rifle over his head and smashed its butt into the bottle. The glass shattered and Jansen fell over with a grunt. Sheer stupidity. But we ran across to find out what had happened, Lüttke asked what the hell he was playing at, and then we were all shouting at each other again.

Jansen had pulled his knee up to his chest and was holding on to his ankle. Through a wide grimace he was muttering cunts, arselickers, all the words you learn in the army. Ottermann pulled Jansen's hands away to see. A shard from the bottle had hit him in the ankle, not badly. The glass hadn't stuck into him, just opened the thick cloth of his trouser leg and the skin underneath. Blood was smearing around his ankle and collecting in his boot. In the condition we were in, it hardly made a difference.

Jansen, though, was blinking and scowling and working his jaw to keep back angry tears. In that moment, lying on the ground in torn and dirty clothes, skinny, unshaven, with flecks of mud in his black hair, he looked utterly wretched.

Lüttke barked, Get on your feet, soldier, or I'll have you court-martialled for malingering.

At that, Ottermann lost his patience with him. He swung the barrel of his Russian sub-machine gun hard into one of Lüttke's kidneys. Lüttke coughed and staggered, holding his side. Ottermann aimed the papasha at his face and said,

If I hear one more word from you about anything, I'm going to shut you the fuck up.

Lüttke didn't shut up. He called Ottermann a shit-eating Communist and told him that once he'd got his promotion, he was going to make Ottermann dig a hole for him to shit in every single day.

In my experience, if someone had decided to shoot someone else, you couldn't stop them with persuasion, only by force. And after what I'd just seen, I didn't want to touch another person, let alone wrestle with them. I didn't want to be involved in anything. So I just watched while they menaced each other. But it soon became plain that Ottermann was too level-headed to get anywhere close to killing him.

Himmelsbach was looking after Jansen. He had a luxury with him, an unused field dressing. They were quite primitive compared to what we have today, not elasticated. To get an even pressure on the wound, you had to employ a clever technique where you wrapped the bandage at overlapping angles. You ended up with a cross-hatched diamond pattern, like the outside of an artichoke.

Himmelsbach was more educated than most people in the infantry – I think he'd worked in a publishing house before the war – but he obviously hadn't been shown how to do it. I watched him knot the dressing round Jansen's ankle like a rag around a leaky tap. Ordinarily I'd have helped, but any kind of initiative felt very distant from me.

Jansen was still swearing and leaking tears when Himmelsbach got him up onto his feet. Lüttke said to him, I hoped you've learned your lesson.

Jansen lurched forward and swung a punch at Lüttke, but Ottermann wrapped him up in his big arms and held him steady. And Jansen, held tight, screamed, What the hell am I doing here? What the hell am I doing here?

He seemed so close to cracking up that it settled the rest of us. Himmelsbach put a hand on Jansen's shoulder, and Lüttke said, Alright, alright. You're fine.

Ottermann steered Jansen back towards the tracks, talking to him quietly. Jansen limped along and Ottermann soothed him like he would have soothed Ferdinand, saying, That's right, walk it off, walk it off.

Jansen soon spun out of his grip and jerkily marched along by himself. We followed behind him, trudging in silence until we came in sight of where the tracks were leading us.

It wasn't at all what I'd expected. I'd imagined a big set of working buildings, a requisitioned farm maybe, with lorries coming and going. But it was some kind of ornate baronial hunting lodge, with a roof like a pagoda and a porch held up by carved wooden pillars. Above the entrance was a coat of arms with a pair of fighting boars. And parked outside were a couple of those motorcycle and trailer half-tracks.

Around it all they'd put up a chain-link fence topped with barbed wire. A brown trail churned by regular traffic led out of a gate and away from us. As we went up to the gate and began to examine the lock, someone came out of the lodge, flicking aside the last of a cigarette.

He was a Feldgendarme, an older man to me then, maybe in his fifties. The military police wore tin placards on a thick chain around their necks, like dogs, and were universally hated, among the ordinary soldiers at least. It was they who arranged firing squads or hangings for our own men.

It wasn't lost on anyone that the men they seized had usually been at the front while the Feldgendarmen had been directing traffic and posting notices about regulations. They'd always come back from a firing squad detail saying, 'He held himself very well,' or some rubbish like that, as if they and he had together taken part in some high-flown rite, when in fact they'd just shot him.

A man in the first company I was in, a spotter on a gun crew, was shot while we were still in training for stealing some cartons of pudding powder. The Feldgendarmen kept saying that it wasn't about the pudding, it was about discipline. I suppose they were ashamed. I hope so. As my father would have said, where there is still shame, there may yet be virtue.

As more of us started to desert, the Feldgendarmen would track them down on their way home, and use a rope to hoist them from a tree or a lamppost, so they strangled. They'd hang them by the roadside, to encourage the rest of us, with signs around their necks that read, 'Coward' or 'I was a coward, now I am dead'. I suppose we felt about the Feldgendarmen the way, after the war, other nations felt about the Germans.

This Feldgendarme, in his ironed uniform, looked as if he were in a different army from us. We could see the fold-lines on his shirt. He was built like a baker or a butcher, with a comfortable paunch, the kind of man who has no education but is used to being listened to. He'd allowed himself a well-kempt moustache and, because he didn't have his cap on, we could see loose grey curls receding from the top of his head. He said to us, Boys, you can't be here. Best keep moving before someone sees you. But you can leave that pony behind.

Ottermann said, What have you got in there, old man?

The Feldgendarme was amused. He rolled his shoulders back and said to Ottermann, You've got a lot to learn if you think I'm going to tell you a god-damned thing. Now, shouldn't you be digging holes somewhere for when the Russians come?

Ottermann said, You tell us what the hell you've got in there, old man. We know what you've got. You've got shitting Bollinger champagne, don't you?

What we've got is nothing to you. What unit are you with?

Lüttke jumped in: We're here under orders as a foraging party. Give us a list of—

A foraging party? Are you thick? Does this look like a Polish whorehouse to you? You can't forage from the Feldgendarmerie's stores.

At the mention of stores, all of us on our side of the fence lost our tempers. We crowded up close to the mesh and told him to open the fucking gate. It would have been wholly in pig-headed character for the army bureaucracy to keep mountains of food safely stocked until the Russians came and ate it. The Feldgendarme was rolling his eyes, but Lüttke managed to get his attention and tried to tell him that it was the German soldier's right to eat while he defended the Fatherland. For some reason, it made me want to weep.

The Feldgendarme didn't rise to our pitch of feeling. Some of his colleagues, also older men, were coming out of the lodge behind him. He scratched the side of his jaw, and said, Listen to me, boys. You can all get fucked. So piss off back to your unit, or I'll hang you from—

At that, Jansen lifted his rifle and shot him, right in the chest.

Six months earlier, I think I would still have been shocked. But now the desperate animal part of me barged any more complex sentiment out of the way. We stormed the compound just as we would have a Russian outpost.

Lüttke, Himmelsbach and I trained our guns on the other Feldgendarmen, who were awkwardly exposed on the front steps of the hunting lodge. We shouted at them to put their hands up, and the truth is we would have shot them if they hadn't. They looked flabbergasted, and did what they were told.

I could see them peering across to try and make out whether their comrade was still alive. He wasn't. He'd gone over backwards as if in surprise, the impact of the bullet flinging his arms out wide.

Ottermann and Jansen smashed the butts of their guns into the bolt on the gate. It didn't give way, and as they kept banging at it, the Feldgendarmen began to recover from their astonishment. One of them inconspicuously took a step back up towards the lodge. I fired a warning shot over his head and told them to lie down on the ground. None of them did so.

The bolt wasn't breaking. All Ottermann and Jansen had

managed to do was twist its housing out of shape. They gave up on their guns and started kicking the gate in time, holding on to each other for balance like can-can dancers.

With each kick, the fence rattled metallically and the bolt's housing bent a little further. But I could see the Feldgendarmen whispering to each other. Lüttke said to me, If we have to shoot them all, we do it.

I fired another warning shot over their heads and shouted, Lie down! All of you lie down with your hands behind your head.

But it only seemed to make them jumpier. And a few seconds later, one of the Feldgendarmen made a dash for the lodge. Lüttke reacted faster than me, and unloaded his magazine into him. The first bullets hit the Feldgendarme in the side and under his arm, knocking him over. His head cracked on one of the steps and he tumbled back down them. Lüttke shot him a couple more times as he rolled, to make the point.

The other Feldgendarmen tried to help him, but Lüttke had already reloaded. He shot the corpse again and shouted, Hands up! Stay where you are!

I ran over to Ottermann and Jansen and started kicking the gate in time with them. Eventually, the bolt's housing rattled loose, and at the next kick the gate jumped out of its frame. It swung but was stopped short by the dead man's foot. Ottermann rammed it open with his shoulder, shoving the dead man's legs out of the way, and we poured inside.

Lüttke and I hustled the prisoners onto the grass, took the pistols from their belts and made them sit down facing away from us. They'd got their voices back and were calling us saboteurs, deserters, traitors to the Fatherland. Lüttke felt the need to argue back.

Ottermann, Jansen and Himmelsbach clattered up onto the colonnaded porch. Ottermann made sure of the Feldgendarme on the steps by shooting him again in the head. Then the three of them crouched around the door.

Ottermann had a grenade ready in his hand and shouted inside, We're Germans, come out.

Nothing happened. He shouted the name of our division and that day's password for our section of the front. There was no noise from inside, so he tried, Come out or we throw in some grenades and shoot the rest of your friends.

But nothing. All we could hear was Lüttke bickering with the Feldgendarmen.

Ottermann turned and shouted, Lüttke! I can't hear a god-damned thing! Why can't you be quiet?

I could see his reluctance to go through the door. We needed to carry this through before our momentum ran out.

But Ottermann was mentally strong. He composed himself, then booted the door open while Himmelsbach smashed the nearest window, and they all began firing inside. That elicited some unmistakably female screaming and a babble of Polish. Ottermann signalled for Himmelsbach to fire another blind salvo in through the windows, while he and Jansen rushed the entrance. An instant later, Himmelsbach went in after them.

I was left out in the open with Lüttke and the sitting Feldgendarmen. As the adrenalin faded and the hard clarity of combat began to blur, the knowledge of what line we'd crossed started to settle on me. It was murder. And treason. If we were caught, we'd be hanged. And probably treated badly beforehand. They might arrest our families as well – my parents, my sisters.

There was nothing to stop some blithe motorbike messenger or a supply truck or a whole fully equipped battalion of reinforcements arriving at any moment. I told Lüttke not to use anybody's name. He said, Quite right, otherwise we'll have to shoot the lot of them.

The Feldgendarmen began scolding us again, more vehemently than was wise. They told us we were common thieves, bandits, Communists. They were not so much afraid as affronted – a sign that they hadn't spent the last couple of years in the manner I had. They were old enough to be our fathers.

I took a few steps away from them, to try and see through the door into the lodge. It was too dark inside to make anything out. I listened for the first sound of an engine coming along the track, but I couldn't hear anything except the blood banging in my ears and Lüttke telling the Feldgendarmen to take off their watches.

Under the pressure to be alert, my concentration for once simply gave way. The attention I'd been paying to my surroundings broke off. I found myself gazing up at the clouds and wishing that I could drift free of the ground – just float, peaceful and diffuse, back West to where I'd come from.

Sometimes I felt so far from home that I worried it would never make sense to me again. But now I imagined that it would be so easy; that if I could step through a door into my old life as a school graduate, as in a fable where years pass in a second, no one would ever suspect that I'd been away. I'd pick up my books, go into a lecture, and in return for this boon I would swear never ever to tell anyone what I'd seen on the Eastern Front.

A burst of gunfire rattled inside the lodge and I gave up watching the Feldgendarmen. I ran up the wooden steps, past the dead man and into a soldier's Shangri-La, cosy, dirty and fantastically stocked.

It was an aristocratic living room, jumbled with carved and patterned furniture. Everywhere were colours long unseen: dark burgundies and a dusky orange that startled an eye used to mud and rubble. There was a Persian rug on the floor, worn down to grey fibres in front of the armchairs. The walls bristled with the yellowing tusks and antlers of stuffed boars and stags, mounted as close together as their bonework would allow. A couple had been hit by stray bullets and were leaking puffs of white stuffing.

More bullets had smacked into a mirrored drinks cabinet, shattering glassware and sending bright shards tumbling among the bottles and beakers. On one of the sofas were two frightened and teary young Polish prostitutes in lace-trimmed nightgowns they must have taken from a cupboard. Crumpled and face-down at the foot of the stairs was a newly dead Feldgendarme, his neck folded back at a fatal angle. He must have broken it after being shot. Killed twice over.

And everywhere else, behind sofas, stacked in corners, under tables or open on the floor were crates and crates of food and drink.

Ottermann was trying to interrogate the trembling Polish girls, saying, *Nemetskiy soldat? Nemetskiy soldat* [German soldier]?, and pointing at the ceiling. But the others had already given themselves over to the crates. Jansen was pouring a tin of condensed milk into his mouth, his back arched and his eyes closed in bliss. Himmelsbach had found a bottle of Napoleon brandy and was drinking it slowly, almost absent-mindedly, the light of some other time playing across his face.

One of the crates had a short crowbar lying across the lid; I grabbed it and started levering everything open. It was a bona fide miracle. There was more than we could eat, more than we could carry. Italian sardines, French cheese, rollmops and dried fish from Scandinavia, tinned peaches from Greece, sacks and sacks of firm, hale potatoes – the last edible booty from occupied Europe. And not just that but real cigarettes, fancy drinks, a crate of whole salted hams packed head to toe.

I was so overwhelmed I started laughing. There was a moment when choice made me helpless. Then I took my bayonet and hacked open a tin of rollmops, which had been a treat for me growing up. Just the smell while I was getting the tin open made me feverish. And once I did . . . I can still taste it now.

After three and a half years of unseasoned cabbage soup and millet mash, food so grey, so completely without flavour, that even famished bodies reacted against it – after that, this complexity of tastes, the sweet tangy fishy freshness; the soft, bitter onions; the texture of a real fish, with white flesh and on the back a glistening strip of black and silver.

Afterwards, in captivity, I used to dream about those mouthfuls. I'd sometimes wake up in my bunk, lost out there in the depths of Russia, perhaps for life, with the taste of rollmops on my tongue.

I ate every herring in the tin and drank the briny vinegar they'd come in. It took about a minute for my stomach to cramp, and then I lurched outside to throw up on the porch. I emptied myself out in long heaves, the rollmops having barely landed before they were hurled back up again.

The truly appalling smell of the puddle I'd made and the sight of the dead Feldgendarme sprawled across the steps cut through my rapture. My head cleared. Lüttke was yelling at me, insistently telling me something. I pretended not to have heard, and went back indoors.

Ottermann and Himmelsbach were shoving fistfuls of food into backpacks. The packs were military size, more like satchels than rucksacks, so they were having to fill bunches of them.

Jansen's attention was on the two Polish girls, who had found some heavy blankets to wrap around themselves and hide their bodies. He was trying to charm them as if they were outside a bar in Warsaw, and Warsaw were still standing.

He told them, Now I know why everyone says Polish girls are the prettiest in Europe. You should come with us. The Russians are only a day or two away, at most. They'll fuck you till you can't walk, and they won't pay for it either. We'll look after you. Come on, take some of this food, as much as you want. We'll have a party.

The girls looked scared of him, and younger than us,

maybe sixteen or seventeen. But well fed. They might have been there for weeks, eating handsomely and tending to the Feldgendarmen. To me then they were so desirable I was almost afraid of them.

I said to everyone, We have to get out of here before someone turns up.

Ottermann said, We know. Start packing. Jansen, leave those girls and go get the horse.

I grabbed some backpacks and began pushing hams into them. I got two hams into one pack, managed to fasten the little clasps and put it on my back. Then did the same with another and put it on my front. Himmelsbach was cramming his bags with bottles of wine and Turkish cigarettes. Ottermann had found a carpet bag that he'd stuffed with so many tins it looked swollen, and he was draping cartridge belts around his neck like metal scarves.

As I scrabbled through the crate the hams were in, I realised that the packing paper wasn't blank. It was scrunched-up Russian propaganda leaflets. 'German soldiers! The war is over! Do not die for Krupp and Siemens!' – that sort of thing. You could be hanged for having one in your pocket. Things were very bad when the Feldgendarmen were using them for packing paper.

I kept filling bags and stuffing tins into the pockets on my tunic. There was a slipping and banging of hooves on the steps outside, and Jansen yanked Ferdinand into the room by his halter. The Polish girls were amazed. The muscular little *panje* pony filled up the space, and lowered his big head to sniff inquisitively at the rug.

Jansen and I grabbed some of the satchels and tried to

put them on Ferdinand's furry back. But we didn't know how to do it. Ferdinand's back obviously didn't have any pegs to hang things on. In desperation, Jansen tried to tie one around the pony's neck, as if he were an enormous St Bernard. At which point, Ferdinand just stepped past us and began snuffling the contents of a nearby crate.

Ottermann said, Holy nutsack, have you idiots never seen a horse before?

I laughed. I couldn't help it.

And Jansen said, What the shit do you want us to do? Here.

He took two satchels and knotted their straps together to make a pair of saddlebags. Then he draped them across Ferdy's back, one bag on each side. Jansen and I got the picture and started tying the satchels together.

Ferdinand seemed unperturbed and carried on exploring the crate with his nose. One of the Polish girls asked us something we didn't understand. And when we shrugged and carried on urgently loading the pony, she brought over a piece of cheese for him. With the heavy blanket wrapped round her, like a squaw in a Western, she fed him the cheese in bits, from the flat of her hand. He munched steadily while she stroked his nose and said things to him in Polish.

Jansen said to her, I know the guy who owns it, the pony. He's right outside. I'm sure he'll let you ride it if I ask him.

The Polish girl didn't understand the words, but obviously recognised the ingratiating tone. She ignored him, and the other one looked scared for her. I would have liked to speak to her, too. But the part of me that would have spoken was too deeply buried.

I started cramming tins into the pockets on my tunic, but it wasn't long before we ran out of satchels and bags, and we were reaching the limits of what we could lift. Eventually, we stopped loading and looked around distraught at all that we would have to leave behind. I said, Are we just going to let this sit here?

Jansen, who was not thinking clearly, said, There are petrol cans outside by the half-tracks; let's burn the whole place before the Russians arrive.

Himmelsbach said, If we start a big fire, people are going to see it. We'll just have to leave it.

I asked, For the Russians?

Ottermann said, Russians need to eat, too.

But then he caught himself and said, No, let's burn it. Why not, eh? It's just going to those pigs anyway.

Himmelsbach said again that a fire would draw attention. But he'd stopped resisting. We'd killed three Feldgendarmen and looted a Wehrmacht store, and we'd caught the taste of a certain destructive freedom.

Himmelsbach went out and came back in with two petrol canisters. When the two Polish girls saw them, they began shrieking. Jansen calmed and shooshed, miming as in charades that the petrol wasn't for them. They seemed to believe him, but stayed in a state of high agitation. The one who'd been feeding the pony, still wrapped in her heavy blanket, started plucking at Jansen's sleeve and pleading with him for something.

I think they wanted to go upstairs and gather their things, maybe their earnings, before we set the place alight. But we'd seen whole nations put to the torch and we weren't going to wait around for some Polish girls' knick-knacks. Now I wonder – perhaps it was photos of their parents, their few souvenirs of childhood, who knows?

In any case, Himmelsbach and I sloshed colourless petrol across the wooden crates, the costly furniture, the Persian rug and the mounted heads. While the fumes rose sweetly around us, the girls dropped their blankets and started grabbing tins.

Ottermann rolled a propaganda leaflet into a taper and we all got ourselves door-side of him. Jansen hauled an unwilling Ferdinand outside and down the steps. Ottermann lit his taper and touched it to a petrol stain on the floor. Even before he'd made contact, a small blue flame leaped up, mindless and hungry. It sliced across the rug like a fiery zipper and began to crackle under a chair.

We hoisted our loot and went outside. The Polish girls were hunching their shoulders forward in their lace night-gowns, their arms full of tins, trying not to let their bodies be noticed. I saw that the Feldgendarmen had fallen silent; now they were afraid. Ottermann shouted at them, One peep out of any of you, and you're dead men.

I didn't want them to come after us on the half-tracks, so I dropped a grenade into each of them. Destruction of Wehrmacht property. But what was one more capital crime? The metallic bangs came as a quick one-two, and twisted the handlebars and steel plating into unusable shapes.

A thick rope of dark smoke started running quickly out of the top of the door and spreading into the sky. I could hear the spitting and cracking of burning wood. Lüttke, who hadn't realised that we'd set the place on fire, went apoplectic. He started shouting that we were out of our shit-god-damned minds.

But it was too late to do anything about it now. We hoisted our satchels and lurched heavily towards the gate. Jansen was playing the chevalier, telling the girls they were free to go home. They didn't really seem to want to leave; I suppose they didn't have anywhere to go back to. With a grin, he asked the one who'd fed the horse for a goodbye kiss. The girl obviously hated it, but kissed him, her arms rigid at her sides, and then the two of them hurried away ahead of us. Two girls in nightgowns going into the woods with an armful of sardines.

We went past the dead Feldgendarme at the gate. He was still lying there with his legs curled up and his arms outspread, as if he were doing some physiotherapeutic exercise. His eyes watched us like a painting's. The colour had trickled out of his white skin, and green and blue flies, like emeralds and sapphires, wandered across his face.

There will be a family somewhere that still mourns him. Maybe they even framed the letter that says he fell on the field of honour. But in me he triggered the euphoria of survival. The war had drawn another round of numbers and again I had not been killed. I felt strong, special, chosen. He was dead, and we were alive.

The hanged village reappears to me whenever I see a bunch of blue-black plums dangling from a branch; that's why I don't eat them. I know that sounds absurd, but it's not unusual. Many men my age, who went through the Russian winters, won't look at frozen meat in the supermarket.

The war in the East was not like other wars. It was not like the fighting in France or Italy or North Africa. It's sometimes said that the war in the East, its cruelty, the genocide, was like hell or like the apocalypse. I've felt those things. But really all they mean is that it exceeded our power of comparison.

How I can maybe express it best is that even now, at the other end of a lifetime, early on a quiet morning in my apartment on a hill above lovely Heidelberg, I can still feel the ache of how I wished to be sent not East, but West, to the war in France.

The soldiers over there were in holidaymakers' countryside in the Loire or the Dordogne, eating cheese and visiting the chateaux. They were trying out their schoolboy French on the mayors and impregnating their local girlfriends. The names of the towns were familiar; we'd learned them in school; we knew people who'd been there before. In the East, the places were unpronounceable; we gave them German names like Lüttke-Stadt or Arschlochburg, and came to hate them.

Everything about the war in France was marvellous. I wasn't militaristically inclined, but our campaign there was astonishing, like a Hollywood melodrama of old wrongs righted. That was how we felt, how I felt. France, the ur-enemy, the envied elder brother, in whose mud our uncles had died at Verdun and Ypres, bowled over in warm sunshine.

There was also a thrilling sense that we were cleverer than them. Or at least Guderian was. His story as we knew it described the classic arc of genius: an obscure officer and student of tactics, Guderian realises early in the 1920s that tanks and aircraft can be employed for a new style of warfare. Instead of having two long lines of trenches facing each other, lobbing shells, you smash an armoured wedge through the enemy's weakest point and race for all the prizes.

No one really believed him until the invasion of France. I'd never heard of him till then. But the newsreels we saw at the cinema were a revelation; the kind of scenes that immediately make everything else look like it belongs to a previous era. Guderian sneaked a tank army through the supposedly impassable Ardennes Forest, ruptured the French lines and then – with what was said to be tremendous élan – advanced so fast that no one in the French or even the German high command had any idea where he was.

His tanks made more ground in a day than the armies of the First World War made in months. He'd conquer one town over breakfast, another at lunch and be in a third by evening. The French were thrown into such disarray that he captured generals who didn't even know their forces were under attack. Then he'd drive all night, and take a couple more towns by morning. He gave his troops amphetamines so they could stay awake and keep driving West, always West, racing the retreating Brits to the Atlantic. His panzers were so far ahead that our infantry would march from dawn to dusk just to get a piece of the fighting.

This was when everyone got to hear and repeat his famous motto, *Klotzen, nicht kleckern* [Don't spatter them; whack them]. We heard the poignant detail reported that, in the invasion of Poland, *der schnelle Heinz* [speedy Heinz] had paused his advance to visit the estate where he'd grown up.

It really was like lightning, the Blitzkrieg. And to us then, it was an enormous release – from the poverty and perceived humiliation since the last war, from the anxiety about this one. I remember going to the shop for my mother and everyone there grinning like idiots, the customers and the shopkeeper breaking into laughter and tears because they were so happy.

Now I think no war is good. But by comparison with the East, the war in the West felt, it still feels, like a relatively clean war, a campaign you could have been proud of if it hadn't been in service of the Nazis.

Even in the time I'm telling you about, autumn 1944, when the tide had turned and the Germans in France were scurrying around under the American carpet-bombing like lice under a lighter flame, it would have been far better to be in the West. The laws of war, that cultivated paradox, were maintained. Atrocities were committed there, too, but they were violations of the rules, not their disintegration.

Defeated armies there were allowed to negotiate terms of surrender; they ate American rations, they smoked American cigarettes and they waited to go home. Compared with the East, the campaigns in France and Belgium were a decorous sideshow, like some kind of formal dance with flags and national costumes, advances and retreats.

I don't mean to insult the honour of the Western allies, who saved three-quarters of Germany and half of Europe from the Russians. I know the invasion of Normandy is cherished in America and England. After all, we had our acts of daring, too, like the airborne invasion of Holland, or Manstein's desperate counter-attack when the front collapsed outside Kharkov. [In Manstein's wilfully blinkered memoirs, he gives his chapter on the French campaign the epigraph, 'Now is the winter of our discontent / made glorious summer'.]

But we Germans know in our bodies – and the Poles, the Ukrainians, the Jews and the Russians know it too – that the war in the East was the real war: naked, pitiless, unrestrained by laws, unmitigated by compassion, a thing of hatred and annihilation. Out of every eight German soldiers killed, seven were killed in the East. And by Russian standards of loss, the Western powers were hardly in the war at all.

In the first year in the East, we Germans starved two and a half million Russian prisoners to death, intentionally. I have seen a man starve to death, I have starved, and it isn't painless, it's not some dull lethargy. It's frantic. Just that, that alone, out of all that was done, was a crime that requires monuments and speeches and days of mourning, but because it was perpetrated in the East, it is hardly remembered.

Our army, or whoever formulated its policies, made a decision to conduct the Eastern campaign not as a rational continuation of foreign policy, but as a war of extermination. We kicked out the supports under the edifice of civilisation, and the East plunged into savagery.

I saw a field hospital the Russians captured that first winter, where they pissed over the patients and threw them out the windows to freeze. When our troops were hunting partisans, they nailed them to the ground alive and chopped them up with shovels. I saw a group of our soldiers whom the partisans had crucified upside down, bursting their eyeballs so the juice ran down their foreheads and stiffened their hair. In Paris, there was prostitution and French girlfriends; in the East, there was rape and murder.

Towards the end, Ukrainian farmers hacked up a hundred thousand of their Polish neighbours with scythes and pitchforks. Poles went on pogroms against the Jews. Czechs kept rape camps stocked from columns of refugees; the Red Army raped so many women that just those who killed themselves numbered in the thousands.

In the East, prisoners of war didn't amuse themselves with escape committees and counterfeit documents; they ate their friends. I saw, with these eyes I still have now, strips of jerky cut from our comrades' thighs and tied to barbed wire to dry. I was lucky enough to be captured right at the end, when the prison camps were survivable.

And we Germans, we who considered ourselves a *Kulturnation*, the heirs to the ancient Greeks, built factories and laid railway lines, employed our industrial and organisational advances, to murder the Jews.

I didn't see the death camps. I didn't know about Zyklon B and the ovens until the end of the war. But I knew that if the people of a ghetto were transported away, they would be worked and killed.

I remember a conversation with two other gunners, quite early on, when one of them had heard that the Jews from a nearby town were going to be shot in the morning. The other thought that it wasn't fitting for the masters of Europe to execute civilians. And the first one said, We're shooting the commissars, we're shooting the partisans, we're shooting the dogs and cats, why not the Jews?

That's how people spoke about it.

Younger generations often make an accusation that of course we knew what was going on, implying that since we knew, we allowed it to happen. I certainly knew about some of it. But in the question of my own guilt or innocence, it was only over the course of years that I began to make out a pattern.

I saw some signs before we'd even attacked the Soviet Union. I had just arrived in the East, in occupied Warsaw, and I went to stand around in a café we soldiers had taken over. That in itself was thrilling for me: to be in a foreign country for the first time, walking the streets as I pleased, going to drink beer with other soldiers in our victors' uniforms.

Some of them had rounded up a group of Jewish women and were making them scrub the floor with their underwear. In those days, women wore slips. The soldiers had made them pull these slips out from under their skirts and, every time the soldiers spilled some beer, the women huddled at the side of the room had to scurry forward and mop it up.

The women were a mix of ages, but all older than the soldiers, who were like me, nineteen, pink-cheeked, big schoolboys, laughing and flushed with what they'd had to drink. Their joke was to pantomime that they were unbelievably clumsy. They'd accidentally jostle each other's elbows or put their beer glasses down on something squint. Then they'd rush in a clamour of outstretched hands to stop the glass from falling over.

But sometimes it would fall. Then they'd cry, Ohhhhhhh! And almost as an afterthought, not really looking at them, they'd click their fingers at the Jewish women to come and scrub it up.

In the café, which I quickly left, unheroic and ashamed, and in the days afterwards, I thought: this is what it means to conduct a war without civility. If you have a rifle, you can be whimsical with the life of whoever doesn't have one. For a long time I believed that although we were near the bottom of the spectrum of how nations behave when they are trying to coerce one another, we were still within its bounds.

I also thought: once this war is won, we, like other nations, will have to think about the abhorrent things some of our millions of people perpetrated while it was going on. I wrongly thought that this cruelty was in the individuals, not, fundamentally, in our system of government, in our culture, in us.

A lot has been said about collective guilt. I can't find any holes in the concept – that even if all you did in the war was serve lunches at a quiet rubber factory in the middle of Germany, your meals fed workers whose rubber went into tyres that were fitted to trucks that carried people to their deaths.

No matter how far you were from it, you incurred guilt, in a greater or lesser portion. The only exceptions were those few who refused to work or answer the draft, whom the country is now so grateful to have had. But if you weren't a hero, you colluded by default. Morally, there was no neutral ground, no safe middle of the herd. And I didn't make lunches; I wore a uniform and fought, to the best of my ability.

So I can't fault the concept of our collective guilt, I just don't feel it. The idea that I'm guilty for things I never saw and had no power over doesn't seem to me to meet the standards of natural justice. But what I do feel, ineradicably, is shame.

Maybe to you that sounds like a trivial distinction. What I mean is that, although I don't think we are all guilty, what happened then tainted everything else, like a patch of rot spreading outward.

The moral system I grew up in, my father's Protestantism, has struggled to say anything sensible about all of this, because it believes that right and wrong is about intentions: that if you mean well, you can't be working evil. But I'm sure most of us meant well. So the best explanation of this shame I've found is from my schoolboy Greek lessons: Oedipus didn't know that his mother was his mother when he slept with her. But what he'd done was nonetheless abhorrent, and he was destroyed for it. There's a pitiless truth in that.

Shame is not like guilt; it's not a matter of reparations. Those people are dead. The ones who were my age, their children and grandchildren were never born. Shame can't be atoned for; it is a debt that cannot be paid.

After the war, when I finally got home and what had been done was everywhere, I remember wishing again that I had been sent West instead of East. Those who'd been in the West wore their shame in a lighter hue. Every time I had that thought, I reminded myself to be thankful that

I hadn't been assigned to anything worse: hunting partisans, maybe, or guarding the transports.

All of which is to say that by the time I saw those bunches of hanged people swaying from that tree, it was plain to me – after three and a half years in which I suffered for my people, and gave of my utmost – it was plain to me that not only were we going to lose this war, it was right that we lose; it was just.

~

Callum: As a kid, growing up in Scotland with only a Hollywood understanding of what Nazis were, and what they'd done, Germanness mainly meant long summer holidays at my grandparents'. It was a big, brown, restful flat above my opa's pharmacy, in the village where they'd finally been cast up.

They'd escaped from East Germany in the early 1960s by jumping off a train that was going through West Berlin. Their pretext for the journey was a holiday on the Baltic coast, near Rostock, so their bags were packed with swimsuits and beach clothes. In West Berlin, they lived in what they described as an American-run refugee camp while my opa tried to find a job. Someone had told him that if he could get across into the West, he could work at this man's pharmacy in Hamburg. He rang the number he'd been given, but it didn't exist. We'll never know why. But there was a jobs board in the refugee camp, where someone advertised a position in a pharmacy at the other end of the country, in this little village near Heidelberg.

So instead of living in a maritime northern city with blue-grey light, dark brickwork, seagulls, fish and mercantile traditions, a place that is Protestant, sober, gimlet-eyed, closer in spirit to London than any other part of Germany, where blond young men drive convertible BMWs to their business management classes, and gaggles of affluent children take sailing lessons on the lake in summer, then go ice-skating in winter, instead of that life, history dealt them a village in the warm, agrarian, cow-smelling south-west.

It's in the thickly forested valley of the River Neckar, a slow, soupy meander buzzed over by beetles and dragonflies. On the hillsides they grow wine and in the summer it was too hot to walk in bare feet on the pavement. There are two churches, one of each, and the people have thick yokel accents that as a child I couldn't hear, because my mum had one. They're cosy, garrulous, deeply settled, and my opa, with his eastern German upbringing and his war-honed austerity, was the stiffest and most proper among them.

To my grandparents, this contrast with Hamburg was the acceptable anecdote for expressing how Versailles, Nazism and Barbarossa had whirled them around like bingo balls in a spinning cage, and spat them out. Europe tears itself apart, a note is pinned to a corkboard in Berlin, and instead of docks we have fields, instead of herring we have venison, instead of being those people we are these ones. Isn't life funny?

When they arrived there, they had a couple of bags of clothes, their swimming costumes, and nothing else. All their furniture was donated by their new neighbours. The churches had organised a collection for the displaced East

Germans. When I arrived, a full generation later, my grand-parents still had some of it: a wicker chair, a massively ugly wooden sideboard. By then they were friends with some of the people who'd donated it. Frau Kuby in particular would come over for coffee and a slice of marbled cake, and ask, Well, Hannes, how much longer do you want to borrow my chair for? Then they'd all laugh and be deeply moved.

To me, that was Germany. It was outdoor swimming pools surrounded by trees; torpid heat settling over drowsy fields; the deep tan of a summer spent outside. It was the homey smell of my grandfather's cardigans; the brilliant white insides of bread rolls streaked with purple plum jam; it was German cartoons and children's books and nursery rhymes that none of my British friends would ever hear of.

To them, of course, in Scotland, in one of what the Germans call the 'victorious powers', Germany meant the Gestapo shooting Richard Attenborough in *The Great Escape*; Ralph Fiennes being a sadist commandant in *Schindler's List*; and the bouncing bomb outsmarting Jerry's defences in *The Dam Busters*. As you'd expect, I think that's ignorant and caricaturish, but no more so than the Germans' idea of Britain, which they call England and where they think everyone is either a tea-drinking lord in a tweed suit or a football hooligan.

I'm not going to yak on about divided heritage or being a bit foreign in both countries. That story's been told enough times already. Whether it's Italians in America or Indians in Bradford or anyone anywhere else, we all know how it goes: my grandparents were foreigners! They ate funny food and said funny things! Between them and me something was lost, but I can't quite put my finger on what!

That said, as a child, I wasn't exactly thrilled that everyone's Christmas celebrations involved watching movies in which men like my granddad got killed. I was too young to even come close to grasping the enormity of what had been done by Germans, or to be ashamed of it. Instead I resented the ignominy that clung to them.

I had a poorly understood sense that the facts of victory, defeat and genocide had turned the twentieth century into a black and white morality tale: the Germans were odious, the Brits plucky, the Americans stupid but useful, the French at least had the Resistance, and all the other Allies had generally done their bit. So I was very susceptible to factoids that seemed to draw the black and white closer together; for example, that the last defenders of Hitler's bunker were French volunteers, the Waffen SS division Charlemagne, who were executed by the French Army. Or I rehearsed the complaint that targeting civilians was a hanging offence when committed by German generals, but an unfortunate necessity when done by the Brits in Dresden or the Americans in Tokyo.

Incidentally, my oma was in Dresden the night it was firebombed, in a cellar with a pregnant woman who went into premature labour from the stress. Later on, when I knew her, my oma had bad lungs that finally killed her. Was it because of the pulverised brick she inhaled that night? Who can say? My grandfather doesn't mention it. I guess there's only so much suffering you can fit into a single story. Human lives, of course, don't work the same way.

Since my childhood I've started to understand, as much as a person can, what was perpetrated in Germany's name. And although you could legalistically tease out varying degrees of culpability, I've got no taste for it. Shame has gathered, like a mulchy spot on an apple. When I watch a war movie, or *Band of Brothers*, where Damian Lewis and the other British actors playing the 101st Airborne stumble across a death camp in the south of Germany, I don't share the righteous distance that lets the audience think, with disgust or anger or whatever they think, look what *they*, the Germans, have done. Instead, as the paratroopers drive their truck through the woods and I can see what's coming – because it's almost the end of the series and they can't not mention the Holocaust – I feel a kind of tense embarrassment, like a shameful secret is about to be revealed.

Why should that be? I was born four decades after it happened, in a different country. In more solipsistic phases, as a younger man who didn't get on with his parents, I probably would have said that it was nothing to do with me. But as I've got older, I've started to feel this odd sensation of connectedness, first to my family and – much, much more distantly – to nations.

It's like there's some kind of constant invisible exchange of sub-atomic particles between the members, like gravity, drawing them together. When the Germans win a football match, as they often do, I don't just feel pleased for them; I feel pleased with myself. And when I watch *Band of Brothers*, I feel the heat rising in my own face.

All this is why I asked my opa about his time in the war. I'm sure it would have been different if I'd actually grown up in Germany. But if you're disconnected from a nation's everyday collective life, you fall back on symbols, kitsch and world history.

So I didn't ask him about his patient, clever construction of prosperity once he'd made it to the West; how he worked himself free of loans and mortgages; that refugee story of the long, laborious road upward from the tent to the retirement hotel on the hill above Heidelberg; nor about how they jumped off a train going through West Berlin; nor about how he and my grandmother met, nor their absorption into the tight idiosyncratic life of a village, nor even the death from illness of their first son; I asked about the war.

To be fair to myself, it wasn't irrelevant to understanding him. World history impinges more on some lives than others. Because I was born in the 1980s and not the 1920s, the worst my times have done to me is lose me my first job, in the 2008 financial crisis; they've never sent me to Russia to dig holes and kill people.

~

We decided not to go back to our unit right away. If anyone asked where we'd been, we'd just say we'd run into some Russians. The way things were disintegrating, they'd probably just be glad we'd come back at all. And, pragmatically, we wanted to eat the loot before it incriminated us. But it suited us to have a pragmatic reason.

Sometimes after combat, you get a soldier's joy that rises higher than anything else I've experienced. Forcing our way through the thick pine woods, I had a very strong sense that my survival was no accident; that I had survived because I was a special man, mighty and invulnerable. And I understood that if it had gone another way, if death had tapped me on the shoulder instead of the Feldgendarmen, it wouldn't have mattered at all. It wasn't that death had grown smaller; rather, I had grown so much bigger in its presence. I felt enormous, jovial, open-hearted, a man-mountain, roaring with laughter because the sky is falling and we are all dead men.

We'd felt how it was to act of our own volition: we'd killed the men who were supposed to subject us to the army's discipline. I was not Oberkanonier Meissner, obeying orders on my few metres of a collapsing front, but a free man, on the loose in Poland with a rifle and a mind of my own.

Anything anyone said made me laugh, and it was the same for the others. Ottermann began mocking Jansen for trying to charm the Polish girls. He did an impression of Jansen cooing and strutting and saying, Oooh, the Russians are coming! You'd better run away with me! I'll look after you, Magda! Ooh, ooh, oooooh!

Then we all started doing it, bowing and blowing kisses and yoo-hooing to passing trees and imaginary Polish beauties. Jansen play-acted the girls, simpering and terrified, and tried to hide behind the pony. Lüttke laughed so hard he bent double and slapped his thigh.

Himmelsbach pantomimed a pompous Feldgendarme shouting at Jansen, Halt! Come back here! I paid in advance!

I joined in too, pretending to be a leering Russian, grasping at Jansen with groping fingers and chasing him around the indifferent pony till we both fell over laughing. I felt a sense of genial bonhomie, of universal brotherhood, as if all men were friends and that, if he could, the Feldgendarme we'd murdered would clap us on the back and laugh about how we'd shot him, because it was only part of this harmless rough and tumble we were all engaged in.

Even the constant background knowledge that we'd invaded a country that was now destroying us seemed no more than a boisterous joke, a pratfall, like a man trying to kick a cat and tumbling on his arse.

Eventually we'd had enough of pushing branches out of the way and decided that we'd gone far enough to be safe, though, as it turned out, we can't have travelled far at all. The ground was springy with moss and rose in lumps over decaying logs. Ferdinand had to be encouraged to keep picking his steps through the mess underfoot. It made for slow going.

We started looking around for a good spot to camp in. There wasn't much under the trees for Ferdinand to eat, only moss, ferns, pine cones and masses of reddish-brown needles. So we carried on to try and find something for him. Here and there among the crowding pines' dark green coats we'd see a vertical spray of red and orange from a solitary birch. And in the end we were relieved to break onto a small clearing with a patch of scrubby grass that Ottermann said would be good for the pony.

It also seemed well enough hidden for us to light a fire once it got too dark for the plume of smoke to show. After all, we said, we'd already lit a bigger fire down the road, and if the Feldgendarmen turn up, we'll just let them have their way with Jansen.

We dug a shallow pit, like a sunken frying pan, to put the fire in later, and collected up some brushwood. Then we laid out our trophies like hunters for a photograph: tins with tins, hams with hams, and so on. Himmelsbach tried to line up the bottles in a row, but they kept tipping over on the uneven ground. With the rest of us telling him to hurry, he finally managed it, gingerly lifting his hand off the last one to see whether it would stay put.

Lüttke wanted us to say grace. It wasn't outlandish to me, but Ottermann just said, No, we're going to have a toast. Himmelsbach, I'm sorry but we're going to need those bottles.

Everyone laughed again and Himmelsbach mimed being a snooty waiter, displaying a bottle of cognac in his hands, label upwards, and asking, Would sir like to try the wine?

Ottermann didn't know the game, so just said, I'm going to do more than try it.

He pulled out the stopper, lifted the bottle and declared, To the high command of the German Army, and to the Greatest Field Commander of All Time, Adolf Hitler, whose wisdom and military genius have led us to this feast.

Before we could shout hurrah, Lüttke interrupted. No, he said, don't blame the high command. It was Hitler interfering that's messed this up. If it wasn't for him telling the professionals how to do their jobs, we'd have won this war already.

Alright, said Ottermann, shaking his head a little. Fine. Not to the high command then, even though I'm not convinced they're so brilliant. Just to Hitler and his friends, whom we have to thank for all this.

Now we shouted hurrah, even though Lüttke grumbled a bit, and dug in. It doesn't tell you much to hear that some people once enjoyed their food, but it makes me happy even now to remember it. We might have been on an Alpine hiking holiday before the war, with a lunch packed by the chefs of a grand hotel. For once, nobody spoke: we were stuffing ourselves.

I used one of the spoons I'd taken from the ashes of the village, and didn't feel guilty about it. In war you soon learn that objects don't really belong to humans. They have lives of their own, travelling from place to place with various people, and outlasting innumerable supposed owners.

Our stomachs could fit so little that it was soon over. One by one, with sighs and groans, we rolled away from the feast and lay there gasping like landed fish. Himmelsbach lit a cigarette and tossed over the packet and the lighter. I hadn't taken up smoking despite four years in the army, but I clumsily lit one, and was content.

Himmelsbach was stretched out languidly as if on a chaise longue, one elbow propping his head. I caught his glance and he lifted his eyebrows as you do when you find yourself accidentally eye-to-eye with someone you hardly know. He said what he was thinking: I might catch up saying grace, since we didn't say it before eating.

Not knowing what to make of that, I said, Of course.

He sat up, bowed his head, crossed himself and started to mutter in Latin – a Catholic prayer. I would have liked to speak to him about it. This was home turf for me; after all, my father was a minister, albeit Protestant.

There had been more educated people around when I was still in the artillery, because you had to be able to do the maths for calculating trajectories. But they'd been rare since I'd become a footsoldier. And the army can be lonely at the best of times. Himmelsbach, I think I said before, worked in a publishing house before being drafted.

He was older than me, around thirty perhaps, and reserved. I imagined that he was doing what I was doing – trying to keep back a part of himself from what was around him. Carried by the mood of bonhomie, I was going to talk to him. But I couldn't interrupt while he was praying, so I rolled onto my side to join in with the others.

Lüttke was eating again and telling a story at the same time. He was chewing in high-speed bursts, then manoeuvring his tongue through his full mouth to keep speaking. His story was about Max Schmeling, whom he claimed a friend of his had met in a hospital in Athens in 1941.

~

Callum: This Max Schmeling was a German boxer whose career was tinctured with the absurd, but who nevertheless emerged from it, and from the era, with more dignity than most. He famously became world champion when his opponent was disqualified for punching him below the belt. He also had a ridiculously old-time ring name – 'The Black Uhlan of the Rhine', uhlans being an especially dashing and intricately dressed type of cavalrymen, who became obsolete thirty seconds into the opening charge of the First World War.

The Nazis loved him because he was literally a white German winning prizes for beating up black guys, and wanted him to be a propaganda mascot. Schmeling said no. From what I've read, I don't get the sense he was a political person; I think he did a simple but extraordinary thing and declined to feel overawed by the power of the state.

So they sent him to the army, to die a hero's death for the newsreels. He parachuted into Crete during the German invasion, but badly injured his knee, and that was that. He survived the war and afterwards some old friends from his time boxing in America got him a concession importing Coca-Cola into Germany. He died old and rich, in the late Nineties, with a stadium named after him.

~

Lüttke said, My friend got in by telling the nurse he was visiting one of the other soldiers on the ward. So the nurse takes him over to someone he's never seen before, all wrapped up with a broken shoulder, and asks this patient, Do you know this man?

My friend thinks he's going to be thrown out, but this patient says, Oh, hello there, sit down, sit down. Yes, nurse, of course I know him. And once the nurse has gone, it turns out that people are always coming to see Schmeling. The price of a visit is two packets of cigarettes. One for the patient and one for the nurse. Isn't that good?

Lüttke broke off another piece of sausage and ate it. He

had to chew for a long time before his throat would let it go down. Meanwhile Jansen and Ottermann, despite himself, waited for him to go on. After a moment, Ottermann rolled his eyes and started unlacing his boots. But he kept listening.

Once Lüttke had swallowed, he winked at Ottermann and said, So my friend hands over the cigarettes and this patient points to a curtain. My friend pokes his head round it, and there's Schmeling, right there, lying in bed, just reading the paper.

Now, it's not what you'd expect, photographers, flash-bulbs, lots of flowers round the bed. None of that. He's just there in his underpants with his leg in a cast. A forty-year-old man. And you can imagine what a Greek hospital is like, just some smelly shed painted white.

My friend's disappointed, as you would be. Schmeling looks up at him and says, Yes? And my friend says, Are you Max Schmeling? Schmeling says yes. And my friend says, I bet you gave it to those dirty Greeks, didn't you? I bet you gave it to them right in the kisser.

And Schmeling says, Hardly, hardly. So my friend says, You mean you didn't even fight any of them? Schmeling shrugs and goes back to his paper. So my friend says, You useless bastard. I'm glad I only paid two packs of cigarettes to see you in here, and not what it would have cost me to see you in the ring.

Lüttke, Ottermann and Jansen started laughing, even though Ottermann put his face in his hands and said, What's he supposed to do, you idiot? Uppercut all the Greeks one at a time?

Lüttke was unperturbed and said, I don't think he needed to get hurt right away. What did he do all that training for?

Jansen, shy but proud, said, I've seen Schmeling box, in Hamburg. I mean, I saw a training session. My mum wouldn't let me go to the fight.

And I joined in the conversation by saying the only thing I knew about Schmeling, the thing everybody knew: Isn't it funny that he got to be world champion because someone hit him in the – because of a low blow?

This comment didn't go over as I'd hoped. Ottermann, Jansen and especially Lüttke were outraged by this smear on Schmeling. All three turned on me, competing to give me the soundest telling-off: Schmeling couldn't help it if the other man was a dirty fighter; he could only beat who was put in front of him; he'd defended that title against so-and-so; his record showed such-and-such; it was mean-minded and disgraceful to bring that up, and so on. Lüttke even said, Isn't it a bit strange that you've been at the front so long, an educated man, and you're still only an Oberkanonier? Isn't that a bit suspicious?

It's not very pleasant to be harangued. And as I tried to mollify them, I became increasingly self-conscious. I could hear my voice next to the others'. Lüttke spoke the jagged Berlinerisch of cab drivers and street traders. Jansen had the related dialect of the Hamburg docks, and Ottermann spoke a broad, agricultural Frisian that would have been comical in someone else. By comparison, my voice sounded as proper as a cloistered schoolboy's. In the end I just held up my hands, took it all back and said I obviously hadn't understood.

They gave me a few more dirty looks, and a dirty phrase or two, and went back to talking among themselves. They were reliving Schmeling's years of triumph in the Thirties, standing up to demonstrate immortal hooks and crosses from the great fights of the past. Lüttke, with his overgrown imperial mutton chops and his rotting cloak, made Jansen jab him in slow motion so he could show off a world-beating counter-punch.

I tried not to attract their attention again by watching them. And I avoided looking at Himmelsbach, in case he'd noticed what had happened. Instead I just rolled onto my back, stared up past the wavering tips of the pine trees at a grey-blue splodge of sky, and wished I was home.

I must have slept for several hours. I dreamed of the village we'd seen hanged from a single tree. My mind has kept that picture, like a fuzzy slide I can hold up to the light, even now. The most merciful aspect of surviving a war is actually how much of it you forget.

Between the war and captivity, I was in the East for seven years, from shortly after my nineteenth birthday until I was twenty-six. Innumerable skirmishes and operations, long months of campaigning, whole terrible mechanised battles like a war between hammers and anvils, must have dissolved from my memory. As an artilleryman you kill a great number of people. There must be many I killed on days I don't even remember. Almost all my life has happened since I got back.

When I was first released, I didn't consider that over the years the war would quietly pack up many of the rooms it had occupied in my mind, and leave; on the contrary, everywhere I looked within myself, there it was. I thought, I'll never speak a word of Russian again, I'll never look at Russia on the map, I'll make myself forget, I'll forget everything, and if I hear that country's name in conversation, I'll close my ears and walk on. I did that for decades.

But then, when we moved to Heidelberg, in 1994, one of the cleaners was Dasha, a Russian who hardly spoke German at all, and it turned out that remembering what I'd learned in captivity had become a pleasure.

Nothing in us stays constant. Our minds are not an archive; everything is always being re-digested by the present. Memories fade; my scars get paler every year; grass grows back endlessly over scorched earth.

Not everything can heal, especially not in such a short span as a person's life. The memory of that village and that tree, and what came afterwards, is as sharp to me this morning as it was the day after it happened. But I wonder, if medicine progresses so that we live for two hundred years, or three hundred, whether at some stage the inner work we do on those things would eventually be complete.

The worst traumas, the firmest beliefs, the most marked traits of character, can all shift and alter as time flows across them; the only thing that stays fixed, or the only thing that has stayed fixed for me, is family.

Your oma and I were family to each other from almost as soon as we met, in a hospital in Dresden in 1948, where she was a receptionist and I was a newly returned prisoner of war. She was the first woman I'd spoken to in more than three years.

Not long after I arrived – I was supposed to walk around the hospital's garden every day to build up my strength – she began using her breaks to keep me company. An act of unforgettable kindness, but not just kindness. She was lonely too.

One of the first times, it was spring already, but there'd been a late flurry of snow. Enough to make a dirty white layer on the ground, with clumps of bright daffodils and bluebells sticking up out of it.

We went along slowly and close together, but not touching. I tried not to let her see how weak I was. Sometimes I'd need to stop to catch my breath, so I'd pretend I just wanted to emphasise something I was saying. Later I understood she saw all that.

As I stopped, it occurred to me how extraordinary it was to see flowers poking up through snow. For a moment, I felt that this had been arranged personally for me, to make sure I paid attention to this day and what was happening with the woman beside me. I suppose I was overwrought: I weighed forty-eight kilos on admission and I was falling in love, so everything was heightened. Nevertheless, to me then it seemed an act of leniency from the Fates, not compensation for the past seven years, because the Fates don't compensate, but an acknowledgement.

I knew then that we would be beside each other until one of us was gone. How could I have known? I didn't. I made a wild assumption, and turned out to be lucky. Since that chilly afternoon in a hospital garden in 1948, the thing that exists between her and me has not shifted. It has not altered, except to grow deeper and more secure. She is the fixed centre around which everything else moves, even now that she's dead. And I would not want to live two hundred more years without her.

~

Callum: On one of her visits to us in Scotland, my oma tried the computer game I was playing, Prince of Persia, and – very unexpectedly – was hooked. It was a basic, early Nineties, 2D adventure in which the prince had to jump over traps, sword-fight Mameluke guards and drink magic potions that gave you special powers. My oma had never played a computer game before, and she had no resistance to its addictive qualities. She'd stay at home while we went for walks, sitting in front of the bulky monitor in my mum's office and pressing the arrow keys to make the prince jump or change direction. At mealtimes, I'd be sent to fetch my oma and she – without turning away from the screen – would say, Yes, I'm coming, I just need five more minutes. Only when I was older did I realise that my parents found it hilarious. Now it's one of the anecdotes that brings back to me how she was.

Dasha, the Russian cleaning lady my granddad mentions, was actually a Russian-German. She was good company, brash, chatty and immoderate. It also made us happy, as it does when people embody their stereotypes, that she dressed like a steelworker's wife from Dnipropetrovsk: a fake-fur leopard-print coat with upturned collar; huge ugly earrings; and hair chopped and dyed the dark purple that's inexplicably popular among Central and Eastern European women of a certain age. Dasha understood herself as a Russian, almost through and through, and proud of it – except that her German blood was a lucky ticket to the West.

There used to be a whole German-speaking region somewhere in the lower reaches of the Volga, with Lutheran churches, neat front gardens and its own insular accent. Like the Romanians in Ukraine, the Ukrainians in Poland, the Poles in Czechoslovakia and all the rest – Ruthenian Slovaks, Transylvanian Saxons, Galicians, the Jews – they were part of the Eastern European plurality wiped out by the world wars and the nation state.

When Germany invaded the Soviet Union, with my opa doing his bit on the howitzer crew, Stalin had the Volga Germans rounded up as potential fifth columnists. Britain sent its own enemy aliens to safe tedium on the Isle of Man. The US had internment camps in California and Arizona for Germans and Japanese.

But as my grandfather might say, things were different in the East. Stalin sent the Volga Germans to hard labour in the mines of Siberia and Kazakhstan, internal exile, where untold thousands were worked to death. After the war, the survivors stayed where they were. There's still an Association of German Community Groups of Kazakhstan, headquartered in Almaty. On their website you can watch camcorder videos of surreal cultural celebrations: blond, blue-eyed Russian-speakers in peasant blouses and red waistcoats, singing very old songs about the Alps.

In the 1990s, with the borders open, as many as a million of them moved 'back' to Germany, after their families had wandered abroad for centuries. One of them was Dasha. Her German was so bad she got the endings wrong in the sentence, 'I am Russian and now also German.' She and my opa were enraptured by discovering that they could communicate in the Russian he'd learned in captivity. They'd have what he reported was a pretty banal exchange – 'How was your weekend?' or 'It's nice that your grandson has come to visit' – and then beam at each other with shared feeling for something no one around them picked up.

They seemed to give each other permission to talk about suffering, albeit always at an angle. Enough was taken as read that they could mention things without having to look at them straight on. He'd tell me how tragic it was that Dasha's grandparents had died on the train to Kazakhstan, or Dasha would explain that my grandfather had had a terrible time in Stalin's prison. My opa would protest and say that actually he'd been very lucky; he was captured right at the end, when conditions were better.

This annoyed Dasha, who'd waggle a heavily be-ringed finger and tell him off in Russian. He'd sigh, flattered, and admit that, yes, it had been terrible. Then they'd beam at each other some more and agree on a profound platitude like, 'Well, life goes on.'

Incidentally, on the question of his weight: in his prime, my grandfather was six foot two and broad across the shoulders. The forty-eight kilos he weighed when he got out of captivity is seven and a half stone. So it can't have been all peaches and cream.

But I think my opa enjoyed the historical irony of their friendship. The story of how he and Dasha came to be there in this apartment complex in Heidelberg, speaking Russian, seemed to him to demonstrate something. That history is a kaleidoscope, perhaps, whose various chunks of coloured glass, some Russian, some German, are endlessly re-combined.

~

I woke up with a pain like cramp in my lower abdomen. At first I assumed it was my bladder. I've had problems with it ever since that first winter in Russia, 1941, when we had no winter clothes and would raid the Russian lines just to take their coats and boots. The cold did something to the bladder, probably caused an infection that eventually damaged the lining.

But the pain wasn't that. As I sat up, wincing, I saw the others squatting among the trees with their trousers pulled down. Each was slightly apart from the others. Lüttke yelled with delight, He's up! He's up! I told you it would get him.

It was the rich food. Our stomachs couldn't cope with it. Soon I, too, was squatting among the trees, each of us with a pale bare bottom protruding from under his tunic. Lüttke had pulled his Romanian cloak up around his shoulders, and it lay across them like a dead animal.

As I blearily tried to rub the hanged village out of my eyes, the delicious stuff we'd gorged on came back out of us. The experience transported Lüttke into a state of glee. To him, this was an instance of priceless locker-room brotherhood. He capered and laughed, whooping when an especially loud gurgle came from someone else, or even from himself. He was yelling, That was a good one, Ottermann! or Watch me go, boys!

Life in the army is founded on indignities, some of which do usher in a sort of fraternal intimacy, but Lüttke really was too much. I tried to push him entirely into the category of things I was ignoring, but he was unignorable.

His brotherly feeling prompted him to reminisce about his rowdy days in the Brownshirts before he was married. Apparently some of them had also had to drop their bowels before their terrific brawls with the Communists. They'd be hiding in an alley round the side of a trade union building, and someone would have to pull down his trousers right there on the street.

Lüttke found this so amusing that he laughed himself silly all over again just thinking about it. He could barely get the words out, and it was some time before he was calm enough to say: It was nerves. They shat themselves with nerves. But the Communists didn't know that. They thought we'd given them a thrashing *and* shat in their alley.

He chuckled again, then sighed, wiping his eyes. And then he just carried on talking, telling us: I had to leave all that behind when I married the meal ticket. My wife's family, boys, they're boss class, real big wheels. Married above myself, didn't I? Of course I did, with a face like this.

Lüttke paused for the jovial ribbing he expected, but none came. He ploughed on regardless: Yes, real boss class. My father-in-law especially is a serious bigwig at the town hall, which is useful now and then, if you know what I mean, but he's also the kind who'd call the police at the first sign of a bit of rough-and-tumble.

Now, I'm not going to let some pork-faced capitalist tell me what to do. Never. But sometimes a man has to put his family first, isn't that right, boys? And it's not my wife's fault how her family is. And after all, not every wife comes with a car you can drive whenever you feel like it, eh, boys?

Lüttke didn't need a response; he just kept talking. I wondered how long he could keep up this monologue and realised that the answer was: for ever. But finally, when he started to lament how the party's high command had ruined the SA, Jansen couldn't take it any more, and told him: Shit on the Brownshirts. They were all sexual perverts with each other. [I'm sure it was put much more homophobically than that.]

I think Lüttke felt hurt, knifed in the back even. His instinct was to retaliate. Still squatting forward with his bottom protruding from under his tunic, he shuffled towards Jansen, saying, What's the matter with you? I see, I see what it is. You're a lying Communist *Drecksau* [dirty pig] and if I'd known you in those days I'd have kicked your head in.

Ottermann raised a big hand as if to gentle a horse and said, Nice and easy, Lüttke, nice and easy. Leave the kid alone.

You can piss off too, said Lüttke.

Jansen threw a scrunched-up ball of paper at Lüttke's head, which Lüttke dodged sarcastically. He picked it up, unfolding the paper, and when he saw that it was one of the Russian leaflets from the hunting lodge, his features curdled. He told Jansen, I'm going to wipe my arse with this just like I wipe my arse with you, you dirty Bolshevik.

And Ottermann, spotting the opportunity to score a point, said, Lüttke, after your days in the Brownshirts, I don't think we want to hear about your arse.

Ottermann meant to tease rather than insult, but Lüttke of course took it badly. Within a couple of minutes, the fraternal bonhomie had broken up, and their reciprocal dislike was back out in the open. The argument with Jansen continued long after I'd decided to take the risk of pulling up my trousers and going back to the picnic.

It can still only have been two or three o'clock. The rest of the afternoon I passed stretched out on the grass like a cat, picking at the leftovers, drinking and examining my feet. It felt like being on leave. But wherever my mind wandered, it kept returning to phrases like murder, treason, theft of Wehrmacht property, destruction of Wehrmacht property.

All the Soviets I'd killed, I'd killed on the authority of my superior officers and, implicitly, *their* superior officers, and so on up the great chain of command, all the way to the head of the Wehrmacht, the head of state and an elected government embodying the will of the people. The Feldgendarmen we'd killed on our own account.

I blocked it out by concentrating on my feet. My socks were disintegrating in my boots and there was a sour cheese stink when I peeled them off. But feet are the infantryman's hobby and an object of daily fascination. They were very white, soft and wrinkled, like vegetables left in the sink. I washed them with water from my canteen, rubbing the dead skin into little crumbs that I could brush off with my hand. My feet felt raw but clean, drying in the open air.

My toes were curling into claws from the long marches, and I massaged them out, to little effect. In the changing rooms at the swimming pool here, I can still see whose feet spent years in boots. As I prodded my sores – former blisters that had rubbed through – Ottermann said to me, You want to put some vinegar on those.

He'd taken off his trousers and was darning them across his knee. His legs were milk white with golden fluff on the calves, and his feet too were swollen and peeling.

I said, Vinegar?

Yes. I used to carry a little bottle of it in my backpack.

I suppose that makes sense.

Or you could use some alcohol.

To disinfect it. I should do that.

Yes, you should. I should too. And it's not like we're going to get through all this stuff any time soon.

For whatever perverse reason, my mind had jumped to the rollmops, which were pickled in vinegar. As I hunted through the loot for another tin, Ottermann said, No hard feelings about before, right? About Schmeling? I think everyone was just a bit wound up. And you know what, you're right – it is funny that he got to be world champion by being punched in the balls. So yes, no hard feelings?

I said, Of course.

Good.

He nodded to himself, then asked, Do you think they'll come after us?

The Feldgendarmen?

Yes.

They'll want to.

Yes.

After a moment in which I hacked open a tin of rollmops with my bayonet, he said, They'll have to find us first.

This was not a conversation I particularly wanted to have. To think about tomorrow could not lead anywhere good. And it wasn't that I had hard feelings so much; more that they were still a little tender. I said, So you reckon I just pour the vinegar onto my feet?

You maybe need to rub it in.

I sniffed the tin and my abdomen convulsed. But I attentively poured the fishy juice on to one foot at a time. The sores stung, and the smell was vile, but it felt therapeutic, like a purgative. Ottermann and I chatted a little about the interests all soldiers share: our feet, the state of our boots, and minor injuries we could show each other. It was surface conversation but pleasant, and limited the Feldgendarmen to the back of my mind for a little while. I hoped we wouldn't have to disguise ourselves by jettisoning the food and dispatching the pony.

Himmelsbach brought out a comb he'd swiped from the hunting lodge and gingerly tried to ease it through the thick black mat around his mouth. The spindly metal tines bent with the strain. So he carefully scratched across the top of the mat, unpicking a few strands, and then a few more. Lüttke called across to him, Hey, who are you making yourself pretty for? Those Polish whores are long gone. It's just this pair of Bolsheviks now.

And Jansen, with a burst of keen longing, said, Oh God, why didn't we fuck those girls when we had the chance?

Himmelsbach ignored all this so perfectly I wondered whether he really hadn't heard. He just lay on his back, smoking and combing his beard.

I didn't know what he was thinking about, but as the hours passed, the rest of us grew despondent, and started to think about the homes we hoped to see again.

Lüttke tried on the watches he'd taken from the Feldgendarme and started talking again between mouthfuls of food he cut with his bayonet. He was saying, What this bread could do with is some good Berliner Schmaltz. [Schmaltz is rendered goose or chicken fat, which you smear on bread. It's very rich, hence: schmaltzy.] I know the place that does the best Schmaltz in Berlin. Used to be a Jewish place. But you should go there and mention my name. They all know me there. Everyone knows me there.

He wasn't particularly aiming this at anyone, more just talking out loud. I wound my own round brass watch and checked it every few minutes to picture what my family would be doing. The army always stayed on German time, even on the outskirts of Moscow. And at this point of the afternoon my father would be making the rounds of his parishioners, visiting the widows. My youngest sister, Gisela, would be coming home from school. Regina had enrolled at university while I'd been away; what she'd be doing was a blank.

My father had given me the watch when I was drafted: a standard gift for new recruits. On the back he'd had engraved, 'Love your enemies, bless those that curse you, do good to those that hate you.' It always prompted an objection in me: that you could only have ideas this simple if you refused to carry a gun. But I was glad to be reminded of him. No one around me thought like that.

And now that I'm older, I see a whole tissue of meaning in it. After all, it doesn't say that you shouldn't have enemies, just that you should love them. Those are the kind of mental inversions my father brought me up on. As I said, you would have liked him. He had an untainted heart.

I had about half a dozen letters from my family in my breast pocket, numbered so that we'd know how many had gone missing. The Feldpost had all but broken down. I'd decided to make this batch last as long as I could, and only open one every week or so. Hundreds of times a day I fretted that I'd be killed before I'd read them all, but I kept to my regimen.

I took out the little stack from my inside pocket and turned the envelopes in my hands to check for stains. The paper had gone soft and greasy, but wasn't wet. One envelope was thicker: Gisela, who must have been around sixteen, was sending me a book in sections.

She would post about twenty pages per letter, as many as could go in under the weight limit. Her idea was that she would read the same sections in parallel and we would write to each other about what we made of it.

I liked the concept, especially because I imagined it would help with her schooling, but it was a complete failure. Most of the sections didn't arrive, and the book itself was the wrong choice. It was Rilke, *The Cornet*. Someone must have told her that it was a good story for soldiers. I'm not sure I could have read anything by then, except perhaps the very lightest, most shimmering escapism, but I certainly couldn't read that.

[*The Cornet* was a bestseller in Germany during the First World War. These days it's hard to read with a straight face. It's about an idealised young soldier who goes off to fight another Asiatic horde, the Turks. On the way to battle, he has a night of passion with a rich, beautiful older lady who finds this pallid teenager irresistible. Unfortunately, the Turks attack her castle while he's in there. He rushes out heroically and dies a glorious death, presumably still in his PJs.]

Poor Gisela! We've still never spoken about it. I decided not to open a new letter and re-read the last one instead. My father had written that the son of one of the neighbours, whom I'd last seen as a child, had been exempted from the draft to study medicine. I should have been glad for him, because the last pathetic wave of uniformed schoolboys was expended merely for a gesture of defiance. Some of the recruits were so young they gave them bonbon rations instead of cigarettes.

But I couldn't be pleased, I was too jealous. Each time I re-read it, I thought that it could have been me starting my studies. Nevertheless, even jealousy tasted better than the war, and I read and re-read, sucking the marrow from the bone.

When I looked up, Himmelsbach was writing a letter in minuscule script, to make the paper last. Jansen was talking to Ottermann about his mother back in Hamburg, saying, She'll be fine. Even if her building gets bombed, she's got cousins all over the city she can stay with. She'll be absolutely fine. My granny was one of thirteen, so my mum's got so many cousins, and aunt and uncles and everything.

And you'll always need bakers. Even the Americans are going to need bakers when they come. It's a job you can't learn just like that, you know. She's got a skill people need. And the good thing about working in a bakery is that you get to take the last rolls home with you, straight from the oven. So in winter, you can hold them in your pockets to keep your hands warm.

Jansen's voice was sinking lower and lower, like the murmur people use in church. Eavesdropping, I had a vision of a stout little woman with a shopping bag picking her way through a deep canyon of heaped rubble, blackened buildings and persistent fires. I was glad my family were not in Hamburg.

He murmured, What's bad for her though is that my dad got killed in France, right at the beginning, when no one got killed. I don't know how he managed it. Maybe he thought he couldn't be killed because he was in the last war. Or maybe he thought he could show the younger guys how to do it.

Ottermann said, He probably just got unlucky. Anyone can.

Jansen nodded deeply a few times, his face twisting. When he spoke again, it was so hushed that even in the quiet of the woods I had to make an effort to hear it: I've just got to make sure that everything's organised for her. One of her cousins lives in Buxtehude. There's nothing there for the Americans to want, so she's moved all her furniture over. But she needs to move her bank account as well, and I don't know how to do that. I don't even know what happens. If the Americans blow up the bank, what does that even mean? Is the money just gone? Her pension?

Lüttke, who'd apparently also been eavesdropping, threw out a comment: I worked in a bank. I know what happens. If it gets blown up, all the records will be gone. Poof. People always think banks are so dependable, but really it's just a building with lots of bits of paper in it.

Jansen sucked in air, startled, and said, What? You used to work in a bank?

Berliner Sparkasse. Deputy branch manager. I wouldn't be surprised if they give me the top job when I come back with my veterans' medals.

Himmelsbach looked up from his letter and said, You think you're going to be wearing your medals from this war?

Why wouldn't I? I've earned them, haven't I?

Himmelsbach tensed as if to say something, then relaxed again and went back to writing.

Lüttke didn't let it go. He said, What? What's your point?

Hold on, hold on, said Ottermann, trying to pre-empt the argument. Does this mean you know how to help Jansen with this thing?

Lüttke said to Himmelsbach, I know your type. Funny isn't it, how many intellectuals turn out to be Jews or Bolsheviks.

Ottermann said again, Lüttke, do you know how to help Jansen's mum with this bank account business?

Lüttke eyeballed Himmelsbach a second longer, then turned to Ottermann and said, Of course. You do it all the time when people move somewhere else. But don't think I'm going to help with this kind of defeatism.

What?

It's defeatist. You might as well hang a white sheet out of your bedroom window. You should be ashamed of yourselves.

~

Callum: I actually lived in Hamburg for a year after my degree, for reasons unrelated to my granddad. My then girlfriend moved there to teach in a private law school for pushy young go-getters, and I went with her. It was an unhappy, lonely year, but I liked the city, other than that I found the way it memorialised the Nazi era pretty creepy.

During the war, the place was ground into dust by Allied bombing – the pictures look like Hiroshima – but today you'd honestly have no idea. The old town was rebuilt literally brick by millions of bricks, all just as it was, except with modern plumbing. I'd like to think that putting a whole town's worth of bricks back on top of each other is a feat of human resilience, a display that we are as ineradicable as mould, constantly growing back. But it does also feel quite a lot like pretending that that era never happened, like making two creases in history, in 1933 and 1960, and sellotaping them together.

To be fair, though, what would have been better? I'd rather look at medieval-ish brickwork than a new town in poured concrete. And there is one bombed-out church, the Nikolai-Kirche, that they've left unrepaired. They've got one in Berlin as well, the Gedächtnis-Kirche – the memorial church. The one in Dresden they rebuilt with stone a slightly different colour, so you can see which bits came through the fire.

In Hamburg, I worked on the famous docks, in the Airbus factory. As a project of European friendship, the planes are assembled partly in Hamburg and partly somewhere outside Toulouse. The half-finished fuselages are flown back and forth in cargo planes so fat their sleek plane shape has gone all squat and bulgy, like a children's toy. It's an expensive hassle to fly this stuff around, but the idea is that helping avoid another Franco-German war is worth it.

My job was to coach the managers in speaking English to their French counterparts. We'd walk through the vast, gleaming halls where the planes are made and they'd practise explaining the production line to me. I heard an awful lot of gags about how the speed of work in Germany compared with that in France – to say nothing of the factory near Madrid!

The managers under thirty-five spoke easy, almost natural English with a slight American accent they'd picked up from TV. With them it was about confidence: as a people that abhors a thing imperfectly done – and that easily feels humiliated – they were hobbled by self-consciousness. None would speak without embarrassment until they were convinced that they sounded as English as the Queen (ha!).

So I spent my time saying, 'Perfect! Faultless! Better than me!' and teaching them uber-English idioms with which to crush the imagined hauteur of their French colleagues. 'Zis engine is up ze spout, guv'nor,' and so on.

The older ones, who'd left school before English was such a priority, were as likely to have learned a few horrid phrases of mangled French as anything else. And those who'd grown up in the East before 1990 had learned Russian.

If they weren't on the production line itself, they were allowed to choose what time they came to work. Being German engineers, they all chose to arrive at their desks by seven. For them it meant having the late afternoon free for the sorts of leisure activity that German engineers enjoy, like cycling or barbecuing or brewing their own beer. For me, it meant taking the water shuttle through the harbour at dawn.

What do I know about it, but I imagine it must be one of the last great industrial sights in Europe. The Elbe is as wide as a lake, silvery blue, and jammed with dozens of ships manoeuvring around one another: container ships like tower blocks floating on their sides; sparkly white cruise liners tiered like wedding cakes with balconies and sundecks; stubby tug boats straining like mules as they haul the big ships through the traffic; flat barges pushing upriver loaded with coal; wooden sailing yachts heading out to sea on the morning tide; the harbour police speeding around officiously in their squad boat; and commuter ferries and water buses stitching every point in the harbour to every other. And all of them criss-crossing each other's wakes and honking and tootling, the big ships' horns so loud that I could hear them in my flat a mile and a half inland.

On one side, the river has been peeled into half a dozen quays that run parallel to each other. The quays themselves are hidden by the mist that comes off the river in the morning, but protruding out of it are hundreds of tall red cranes, swinging slowly to and fro as they lift and lower containers off or onto the quayside. The containers are in simple colours, blue, white, yellow or red, and marked with the names of shipping lines, like Hapag-Lloyd or Maersk. They've travelled across open ocean from Hong Kong or Boston or Mumbai, bringing Hondas and iPhones and taking back BMWs and washing machines. And at the furthest reach of the harbour is a newish hangar-like building that hosts a permanent production of *The Lion King: The Musical*, to which an audience of tourists is ferried every night on a special lion-coloured boat.

I used to look at this tableau as the company water bus bounced across to the other side and the sun rose behind the city, making the river's surface shimmer and dapple, and I would think: this is the ingenuity and industry that have made humans top animal; busy, clever, indefatigable, taming rivers and throwing a girdle of ships around the globe. It made me think that if you dropped a troop of naked cavemen on an untouched riverbank, within a few short centuries they'd have organised a town, a trading network and a system of exchange rates for Canadian furs and Sumatran nutmeg.

You'd never guess that within living memory the docks were bombed into a mess of water and shattered stone. But far out on a distant headland pointing towards the sea is a statue remembering the sailors who set off from here and never came back. And on the streets the docks paid for, outside many, many of the houses, they've put in brass cobbles among the stones. Each brass cobble is inscribed with a Jewish-sounding name and that person's fate: murdered in Dachau, murdered in Buchenwald. Where a whole family was taken from one house, you get five or six of these cobbles fixed next to each other. In winter, the low sun catches their surfaces and makes the brass glow, but otherwise you hardly notice them. You'll be looking in a shop window, trying to decide whether your British coat is warm enough for this weather, when you happen to glance down and see the names beneath your feet.

~

Ottermann kept harassing Lüttke about the bank account until evening. He couldn't stop picking at it even though Jansen, who was finding it painful, asked him to leave it alone. He didn't want Lüttke's help. Ottermann said, You're right, you're right. I should just say, you make me sick, Lüttke. You hear me, Lüttke, you make me sick. And leave it at that.

But then he brooded over it until he couldn't keep it in any longer, and came at Lüttke from a new angle. He would say, The woman's given her husband already for the country, don't you think she's given enough?

Or he'd say, The Americans are going to flatten everything anyway, why do you care if she saves whatever she can?

Unfortunately for him, Lüttke loved the attention. He reclined like some oriental magistrate, looking past Ottermann into the dusk and lifting snacks to his mouth. He interrupted to make orotund pronouncements like: What you don't understand, you treacherous little Bolshevik, is that it is beneath my *dignity*, my dignity as a German soldier, to help you undermine the morale of the German people. If Jansen wants Mississippi Negroes requisitioning his mother's apartment and sleeping in his bed – if he's lucky – he can be my guest, but I'm not going to help him do it. And if he's just going to lie down and capitulate like the snotty coward he is, he might as well find a nice spot in the woods, shoot himself, and save the Bolsheviks the trouble.

While Lüttke spoke, I tried to distract myself by grazing on our picnic. But it made me worry about my own family. They didn't have much money to start with. I wondered whether they could buy gold jewellery and bury it.

Himmelsbach plainly had something to say about this. When Lüttke was sounding off, he sat forward, clicking his teeth. But while I was watching, I saw his will to change the thoughts of the others drift away. His gaze disengaged as it does when you stop listening. He rubbed his nose, ran his fingers through his beard, leaving deep grooves, then got up and went over to pet the horse.

Ferdy had been stolidly unperturbed by our increasing fractiousness. He was snuffling the ground and rubbing his neck against the tree that Lüttke had tied him to. One reason we got so attached to animals was that they didn't know there was a war on.

Himmelsbach crouched to inspect Ferdy's sides. On impulse, I went over and joined him. Strange that I still had the capacity to feel shy. I said, He's a good horse.

Himmelsbach's closed expression brightened for once, and he looked amused. He stood up and said, I had riding lessons growing up. Dressage. Showjumping. All that. I'm not sure my instructors would have agreed with you.

It seemed this had come out more negatively than he'd meant, because he hurried to say, But yes, I like him too. I've been wondering whether you could ride him. What do you think?

I said, For show jumping?

Ha! No. I thought . . . this has been such a good day. The food. The brandy. It's made me remember a lot . . . can you ride?

I'd never even met anyone who rode. My family had no contact with the world of luxuries. So I said, It's never really been my sort of thing.

He nodded, weighing up what that meant. Then said, You've been at the front a long time?

I'm in my fourth year.

He waited, expecting me to say something more. I wanted to – to keep the conversation in the air – but there was so much and nothing to say.

So he went on, For me this is my seventh month. Or rather, I had a couple of years in a cultural unit. Violin concertos in army towns. Lots of reading, letters. Not bad really. You could sometimes get a weekend at home. My wife's birthday. In March, I'll have got through a year at the front. And with what happened today – he raised his eyebrows and shook his head – my old life seems a long, long time ago.

These things were what I'd hoped we could talk about. But it was so unexpectedly direct, and I was out of the habit of personal speech. I slowly devised a question: What did you do before you were called up?

Worked in a publishing house. An art publisher.

Photography books, that sort of thing. Married the boss's daughter, if you can believe that. It's funny to think I'll probably never see it again. I probably would have ended up running it . . . But I am going to get on a horse again, aren't I, Ferdy? What a day! What a day. A picnic, brandy and a little trot. It's not so bad, this army life, is it?

It occurred to me that he might ride into the woods to shoot himself. I hoped he wouldn't. To keep us both talking, I broached what I thought we had in common, and said, You know, my father's a minister, so I grew up Protestant, not like you, but we used to say grace before meals. There's almost no Catholicism at all where we live. But so much of it must be the same.

This was not the right thing to say. It disturbed the sentimental mood he was in, like someone bringing up a serious subject while you're trying to enjoy yourself. All he said was, Oh yes.

I didn't read the signs of his unease, and said, My father gave me this watch that says 'love your enemies' on the back. Isn't that funny? Is that what it's like in Catholicism as well?

Himmelsbach made a brief wincing expression as if I'd said something unpleasant. He scrunched up his eyes, then began untying the rope that bound Ferdy to the tree. He said, Oh, I don't know, really.

It varies?

No, I mean I really don't know.

I waited for him to go on and finally, reluctantly, with his back to me, he said, I'm quite new to it. Never that interested before.

He got the rope free, pulling it around the trunk, and as he turned back to me, he said in a bright voice, But now I'm going to get on this horse. I've never ridden bareback before. Only read about it in *Winnetou* [a series of German children's books about a noble Apache warrior]. Indians always ride bareback, don't they? So it must be possible. Better hope Ferdinand knows what to do.

The voice didn't fit his face. His eyes gleamed like pale wax between his combed dark hair and his dark beard. And his mouth hung open, as if his heart were beating double-time and needed air. It was the face of a man trapped in rising water, not yet panicking, but close to panic, and afraid, terribly afraid.

I felt like I was looking down a deep well and seeing him at the bottom, looking up. I wanted to tell him something that would make contact. All I could think to say was that when the war was over I intended to study chemistry. But it seemed too much of a non sequitur, and I said nothing.

I watched while he put his hands on Ferdy's shoulders, to steady him, and cautiously lifted one leg up over the pony's back. He made a couple of hops on his standing foot and then jumped his weight up onto Ferdy. Immediately he was hushing and soothing the pony, who picked up his head and shifted forward a little, but didn't seem concerned.

Himmelsbach's legs were comically wide apart around Ferdy's barrel-shaped frame. His voice still bright, he said, Tell me the truth, Meissner, do you think I could pass for Winnetou up here?

Himmelsbach mimed brandishing a spear and let out a high-pitched, ululating war-whoop. I was still searching for something real to say to him. But it was beyond me. Instead I raised my right hand like they did in Winnetou's adventures, and said, Howgh!

He made a brittle laugh and, with his knees, managed to coax Ferdy into taking a few steps forward. When the pony stopped again, Himmelsbach seemed to consider thwacking him with the end of the rope. But he was worried that that would elicit too much movement, and instead just tried quietly saying, Hiiyah! Hiiyah!

I stared at him lurching forward and back like a child trying to move a wooden horse. In that moment, I had no means of communicating with him. After a while, I went and sat back down, feeling very crushed.

I saw that something had changed with Jansen. He was lying with his face in the dirt and his arms around his head. From the way his back was trembling, I think he must have been in tears.

Lüttke was watching him and making a show of being sceptical. Noticing I'd come back, he said, Well, we've learned all we need to know about Jansen's will to resist.

Ottermann told him, Just leave it. Just, please, Lüttke.

I don't see why it's such a big tragedy. It's only a bank account. How much money can a baker even have in there?

I could see that Ottermann was trying to block him out. Still sitting down, he shuffled himself over to Jansen and put a big hand on his shoulder. He tried to coax him into sitting up, saying, I'm sorry, I should have let it go sooner. We'll make sure your mum's alright. Nothing's going to happen to her. Everyone needs bakers, even the Americans. You said so yourself.

But Jansen shook him off and just lay there, face-down.

After a few more minutes of coaxing, Ottermann gave up. He eased a tin of peaches out from under Jansen, to make him more comfortable, and sat with a hand resting on his tousled hair.

The longer Jansen lay there, the heavier it weighed on the rest of us. Eventually, it made even Lüttke uncomfortable; he told Jansen that enough was enough and he could get up now. But Jansen didn't move, just sometimes his shoulders would shake with whatever was going through his mind.

In the meantime, a dispiriting grey dusk gathered around us. The trees further off started to blur behind a gauzy dimness that thickened like a spider's thread spooled innumerable times. The bright patch of sky we could see high above us was going out. On the page I was re-reading, my father's scratchy handwriting was sinking back into the paper.

I preferred it when real darkness finally closed up around us, and it was time to light the fire. Himmelsbach and I went about it noisily, talking loudly against the deep forest hush. But once it was going and we had said to each other that it was burning well and that it was good to have a fire for once, we each sank back into ourselves.

I watched the fierce glee of the little flames destroying the wood and listened to the sap in the branches pop and spit. The ground under me began to warm up. I wondered, if I was killed, how long my sisters would still talk about me before I belonged to the past.

The despondency started to get to Lüttke, who fidgeted, then went back to stuffing himself with any food and drink that was within reach. Between gulps he glanced across at Himmelsbach and said, Hey, don't you have a harmonica or something? What songs do you know? What about *Alte Kameraden*?

He began tunelessly singing the lyrics to this marching song, apparently not bothered that the rest of us ignored him. After a couple of verses, he lost his grip on the words, so just went back to the opening again. Once he'd done that enough times, he went on to something else.

It just made me sadder, because these songs reminded me of the first, victorious, phase of the campaign. There'd been a lot of singing around a campfire at night, back then: war seen in the lustily heroic aspect of books for boys, a glamorous, grown-up version of hiking with the scouts.

And the songs themselves, the songs, how I hated them – their crude sentimentality, the oompah rhythms and the kitsch *volk*-y lyrics about flowers and maidens and trusty comrades. There was always a beautiful woman waiting somewhere and a solitary soldier keeping watch on the banks of the Rhine or the Volga. These supposed battle songs, marching songs, were really about being lonely and homesick.

Lüttke soon moved on to one of the most thumpingly repetitive tunes in the army repertoire. Some of the lines had a three-beat gap, where you kept time with the sound of marching boots. So it went: 'On the heath there blooms a flower' – stamp-stamp-stamp – 'and it's called' – stamp-

stamp-stamp – 'Erika.' We learned it in training and by the time I'd heard it the first hundred times, I thought I'd never get it out of my head again.

[*Erika* is German for heather. In the song, it's also the name of a sweetheart waiting at home. No Scottish connection as far as I know.]

Lüttke was laughing while he shouted the lyrics. He rolled onto his back and marked the beats by kick-kick-kicking his legs in the air and yelling, Bumm-bumm-bumm. He must have already been a little drunk.

If our situation hadn't been so dire, I don't think these songs would have got to me. But they did. A sentimental melancholy, not all that far from self-pity, started to suffuse my thoughts. I wrapped myself up in my poncho and prepared to go to sleep.

Lüttke kept drinking, singing and capering, wailing a tune called *Glocken der Heimat* [The Bells of Home]. I'm not ashamed to say that I cried then, lying on that Polish earth and thinking of what my life had been used for. I would never be a professor; I would never make great discoveries; my good marks and my aptitude for chemistry would not lead to anything. I hid my face from the others and pretended to be asleep. Lüttke kept amusing himself, and even though it was all rubbish, I was grateful to him and didn't want him to stop.

I wasn't paying attention to what the others made of it. But the next morning, when the damp dawn pulled us unwillingly back into the waking world, Jansen was gone.

~

Callum: When I was a teenager, I'd sometimes see this weakness for melancholy on German Friday-night television. My granddad would have gone to bed and I'd be channel-hopping with the lights off and the volume low, looking for the soft-core porn that's also a German TV staple, when instead of hairspray and implausible moaning I'd land on a studio full of retirees listening to *Schlagermusik*. It's like a German equivalent of American country music, with sets decorated to look like Alpine huts and the backing singers dressed up in dirndls and blonde plaits. The performers are often middle-aged men with mullets and beer guts, old-fashioned warblers and wailers who specialise in nostalgic ballads about saying goodbye and missing home and never coming back to their sweethearts again.

The most famous *Schlager* star now, a tall blonde blue-eyed beauty, is a Russian-German, like my opa's old cleaning lady. She's called Helene Fischer and was born in Krasnoyarsk, Siberia. I don't know how she came to this genre; perhaps it's the obvious thing about trying to be more German than the Germans. But there was a year when you couldn't go into a supermarket there without hearing her biggest hit, a pop crossover called *Breathless Through the Night*, being piped in among the meat salads and fruit liqueurs. When my wife and I went to Berlin for a weekend last summer, to visit a couple of friends who'd moved there for the low-rent lifestyle, it was still playing in taxis and kebab shops.

The specific songs my granddad mentions are now taboo, as is anything with too strong a connotation of that era. They're Nazi songs. They're all on YouTube, though, uploaded by a creepy and deluded subculture, Nazism enthusiasts, the sort of people who run chat forums discussing why Manstein was a better general than Rommel. They're the ones who keep alive the supposedly contrarian publishers still putting out books on how the SS Leibstandarte Adolf Hitler was actually a really impressive elite organisation. I imagine most of them are harmless nerds drawn in by the interdict. But still, fuck those guys.

Their videos get a pretty shocking number of views. The comments underneath are usually from Eastern European skinheads who somehow succeed in believing that the Nazis were on the right track. It doesn't do the heart much good to think about these Poles and Russians who, based on what happened in their countries, are in favour of a racial hierarchy just as long as they're not at the bottom of it.

These war songs, in their taste for melancholy, yearning, what the Germans call *Sehnsucht* – an unplaceable sense of longing – are often barely distinguishable from the Friday-night *Schlager* hits. The one called *Alte Kameraden*, old comrades, invites soldiers to imagine that, come tomorrow, their brothers-in-arms will be scattered or dead. It's pre-emptive nostalgia – nostalgia before anything has even happened. The song was actually written in the 1880s but is now beyond the pale because it was popular under the Nazis. Guilt by association. A few years ago, a *Schlager* star called Heino released a version with the same tune and title but different lyrics. The new text has got less to say about honour and glory, and more about how sweet the wine is at reunions. Nothing ever ends, does it – just turns into something else.

The most popular of these *Sehnsucht*-infused campfire songs, *The Lorelei*, was written a hundred years before the Nazis by Heinrich Heine, a German Jew. The opening lines are: 'I don't know what it means / that I feel so sad.' The Nazis tried to ban it, but couldn't make the ban stick. So in songbooks from the time, it's credited to 'traditional'.

You can never fully divorce the artefacts of the Nazi era from the rest of German culture, uncomfortable though that is. It was the same cloth, but bunched and twisted into a grotesque shape. Stamping some things as Nazi things has its reasons, but it's like stamping the leaves on the surface of a river, which keeps on flowing deep and silent underneath.

Once you realise that, you see it everywhere. The sprig of oak leaves that used to be presented alongside the Iron Cross is now on the back of the euro cent, and I have an oak-leaf-shaped ashtray sitting on my desk. Today's national anthem, sung at football matches, is just the third verse of the old 'Deutschland Über Alles' song. The first verse was banned after the war because it names Germany's borders as the Rivers Maas, Memel and Etsch, which are now in France, Lithuania and Italy, and called the Meuse, Neman and Adige.

East Germany had the same tune but its own words, under the title 'Risen from the Ruins'. And the tune itself was originally written for a completely different set of lyrics: 'God Save the Kaiser'. Like I said, nothing ever disappears. The best go anyone's ever had at making a clean break was probably Germany in 1945. They call it *Stunde Null* – hour zero. But clean breaks don't exist.

~

It wasn't immediately obvious that Jansen was gone. When I woke up, he wasn't there, but he might have been anywhere. Ottermann was lying flat on his back, staring up at the drifting clouds and sucking pensively on one of the plaits in the end of his beard. It seemed an odd mood for such a practical person. But, not having any consolations to offer, I preferred to leave him to it.

Himmelsbach was poking through the satchels of loot, enjoying himself by drawing out the decision of what to have for breakfast. When he saw me move, he said, No coffee, I'm afraid. Wouldn't that have been just the thing?

I nodded and stretched, still too groggy to speak. I felt as if I could have gone back to sleep for a couple of days. My body had had a taste of rest and now wanted a lot more of it. I also had a mild hangover. What luxury. I rolled onto my belly, ran my hands through the wet grass and washed my face with the cold dew. It was very fresh. It would be winter again in less than two months.

I rubbed my eyes, pushed myself up onto my feet and went to empty my bladder. When I came back, I was about to ask Ottermann where Jansen was, but I put this together with his odd mood, and a sudden foreboding held me back.

It was a kind of superstition: that if I didn't say anything, it was more likely everything would be fine. As if you could call things into reality by noticing them. Better to look away. Then maybe his foot would miss the buried mine; the partisans would walk a different route; he'd take the end of the rifle back out of his mouth. And there was no need for these imaginings; he was probably just relieving himself.

But as the morning wore on, this not noticing became ever harder to keep up. I stroked Ferdinand's silky nose, I chatted to Himmelsbach about breakfast, I ate some of our riches, and this unsaid thing kept butting at the border of my mind, trying to get in. Ottermann was still staring up at the sky and I got the sense that he was doing something akin to what I was, staying motionless in case he disturbed something delicate.

Lüttke was still asleep under his cloak, face-down with his head on the crook of his arm. Finally, when I felt that Jansen's absence was as explicit as a scream, Himmelsbach glanced around and said, Hey, where's Jansen got to?

I looked at Ottermann, who said, I was awake just when it started to get light and he was already gone by then.

Himmelsbach opened his mouth to say something, changed his mind, shut it again and ran his hands down his face. His fingers were shaking. I think each of us was picturing the same scene: Jansen slumped under one of these trees, with his rifle in his hands and his brains sprayed out the back of his skull.

I said, Maybe he's just gone home.

Ottermann, who was still lying down, said, Home?

You know, just started walking back to Germany. It's probably only a few days to the border, isn't it, if no one picks you up.

We all considered that.

Himmelsbach said, How far do you think it is? A couple of hundred kilometres?

Ottermann weighed it up, and said, More or less.

I said, Not far at all.

Ottermann thought out loud: If he was going back to Hamburg, he'd have to walk all the way across the country as well. What's that, a few hundred more kilometres. Where's your family, Himmelsbach?

As far south as it gets, near Lake Constanz. Almost the furthest bit of Germany from here. But my parents have an apartment in Munich. If it hasn't been bombed, then, well, that's a bit closer.

Ottermann slowly stood up out of his long immobility and swung his arms around. How about you, Meissner?

Naumburg, my family live in Naumburg.

So you're the closest.

Yes.

Himmelsbach asked us, How many kilometres do you think you can walk in a day?

I said, A quick march is about six kilometres an hour. Let's say four because you're not on the road. Say you hike ten hours a day, that's forty kilometres. But of course you'd lose time because you'd have to navigate, there might be obstacles, you might have to hide and so on.

Himmelsbach said, So, to the German border, four or five days.

At most.

We all thought about that. Ottermann was the first to

come back to the present. He said, Well, I hope that's what Jansen's done. Walking home with a big pack of food.

That took us back to visualising the more likely scenario. Himmelsbach said, Well, we'd better go and find him.

Ottermann and I sheepishly avoided catching his eye. Another corpse to look at. I felt no need to see it. Even after seeing so many, the effect on me still wasn't actually zero.

Come on, said Himmelsbach, we can't just leave him lying around.

And I thought, We left those villagers lying around. I've left an awful lot of people lying above ground. But I didn't say anything, and neither did Ottermann.

Himmelsbach tried to persuade us and we quietly evaded his insistence while dappled sunlight shone on the earth around us and the horse thought his horsey thoughts. It was turning into a lovely day. The small clearing was beginning to feel like a charmed circle, a safe atoll in infested waters; Jansen's corpse could be bobbing about anywhere beyond its edge. For all I knew, when I'd gone to empty my bladder, it had been sprawled somewhere nearby, staring at me.

After a while, Himmelsbach said, Alright, well, I'm going to have a look.

Ottermann and I nodded at him. He hesitated a bit longer, his eyes flicking back and forth between us, hoping we'd change our minds. He said, You're really not going to come?

I shook my head. And I could see that Himmelsbach wished he hadn't committed to this. He wanted to sit back down and relinquish Jansen to the Fates. But fear of embarrassment is a powerful force. So he picked up his rifle, chose a direction at random and strode into the trees.

After a moment, Ottermann said, He'll learn.

But I had no interest in knocking down Himmelsbach to build ourselves up. So I made a non-committal noise and decided to open one of my letters. Ottermann started tidying up, putting the food back in the satchels. I don't know where he thought we were going.

I got comfortable, lying flat with my poncho rolled up under my head, and held on to the letter I'd chosen. I could hear birds here and there in the forest, and Himmelsbach calling for Jansen. I often regretted that I'd spent years in the outdoors and could still barely identify anything but the most obvious trees and plants. Birds I had no idea of. I had a fantasy that after it was over, I'd collect books of ornithology and arboreal science, and gather up the knowledge that I'd trampled through so wastefully.

I teased open the envelope with my thumb, careful not to rip it, and began to read. I was through the letter in a minute, a minute and a half maybe. There was hardly anything to it. I went back and started again, chewing the flavour out of each sentence.

It said that Gisela was taking first aid lessons, along with the rest of her school, and thinking of becoming a doctor. They were doing the lessons in school time, which worried my parents. They thought her education had already been disrupted by the war, so my father was giving her remedial Latin lessons on Saturdays. I tried to visualise every detail – the dark polished wooden dining table, the tablecloth with the geometric border my grandmother had embroidered, schoolbooks, declensions, verb tables, Cicero, my father's teaching voice – it felt as unreal as a children's story.

At some point, I realised that it had been a while since I'd heard Himmelsbach. It must have been nearly half an hour since he left. I looked across at Ottermann, who seemed exhausted. He said, Takes you a while to notice things, doesn't it? I think he must have found Jansen. Let's go get him. Last time he shouted, it was over there somewhere.

I got up, hoping we wouldn't find them laid out next to each other. We hadn't heard a shot, but Himmelsbach wouldn't have been the first to use his bayonet on his wrists. I put my helmet on and lifted my rifle into the ready position, as if for protection against their ghosts.

But it didn't take us long to spot Himmelsbach, by himself. He wasn't dead. He was kneeling on the mossy floor, stripped to the waist, with his tunic hanging from a branch. His hands were clasped in front of his closed eyes. He'd made a muddy patch with water from his canteen and daubed a faint cross onto his chest, where it had clotted among his chest hair. His torso was luminously pale in contrast to his sun-browned head and forearms. You could see from his skin that he wasn't as young as I was. Tears were running down into his beard and he was rapidly muttering an incantation, maybe Hail Marys.

Ottermann said, Himmelsbach. Himmelsbach.

Himmelsbach didn't react, just kept muttering. For my part, as unfair as it was, I found this irritating. Yes, he was in desolation. But so was I, so was everybody. Him behaving like this just reminded me of everything I had to be depressed about.

Ottermann said, Do you think he's cracked up?

I took in the muddy cross on his chest, and said, Maybe. We'd better stand him up.

I didn't want to do anything with him. I'd almost rather have just gone back to my unit. At least there you fired back or you got shot.

But Ottermann and I lifted him from under his armpits and put him on his feet. His legs couldn't support him and he slumped against Ottermann's big chest, sobbing and sobbing. Thank God the muttering had stopped. Ottermann held him upright with an expression of distaste, and craned his head back so that Himmelsbach's wild hair wouldn't touch his face.

Then Ottermann turned him around, so that I could clean off the muddy cross. While I was doing that, he stopped crying, but kept his eyes closed.

I said to him, Chin up, Himmelsbach. It's not the end of the world.

There wasn't much feeling in this statement, and he didn't seem to notice it. Once I'd cleaned him up as best as I could, we put his tunic on him. Some of his things – a letter, his comb, some cigarettes – had fallen out of his pockets, so we buttoned them back in.

Then we held him up between us and walked him to our little camp. By the time we got there, his feet were finding the ground and he could talk again. I said, Your things are in your pockets.

Thanks.

Ottermann asked, You didn't find Jansen then?

No.

Himmelsbach sat down where he'd slept. He now didn't look distressed so much as dejected.

Ottermann marched over to where Lüttke was still sleeping. On the ground near him were a few empty bottles. He must have got a lot drunker than the rest of us. Ottermann said, He should go look for Jansen. He's the one who bullied him. Or we could just cut his throat right now. That might be fairer.

He wasn't serious, but he wasn't joking either. I quickly said, I'll wake him.

With the tip of my boot, I prodded Lüttke's thigh. Nothing happened. I kept prodding until Ottermann said, Kick him properly.

Lüttke must have been half awake for a while, because when he heard that, he pulled his mangy cape over his head and groaned, Shit on yourselves, the lot of you.

I said, Get up, Lüttke. Jansen's gone.

Lüttke went rigid, then rolled over and slowly sat up, one eye pinched shut against the daylight. Rubbing his arm where he'd been lying on it, he avoided the subject and said, I've got pins and needles. But that was a good drink last night, wasn't it? I tried to go for a piss and just fell over. Ugh, I think I might throw up. Why are you all up so bright and early?

I said again, Jansen's gone.

And his rifle's gone?

Yes.

Probably shot himself then, hasn't he? Or maybe the partisans have got him. And you, you fucking lump, just try to cut my throat and see what happens.

Ottermann almost shouted: If it had been partisans, we'd be dead too, you shitting idiot. He's probably round here somewhere, and you're going to find him, and give him a proper burial.

What? Why? If he's dead, he's dead. He'll be better off like that than with the partisans. They'd have cut his dick off and made him eat it.

It's always about dicks with you Brownshirts, isn't it?

Ottermann and Lüttke insulted each other for a while. I couldn't really disagree with Lüttke that there was no point trying to find the body. But I would have been quite happy to see Ottermann make him do an unpleasant job. Lüttke thrashed around like a fish on a line, trying to get off the hook, and asked whether Jansen had left a note. No one had checked.

Still rubbing his forearm, he went over to the things left where Jansen had been sleeping: some satchels of food, bottles, cigarettes. He bent forward, froze, and put his hand to his temple. He said, Ugh, and spat on the ground. Then he started turning the satchels over. Underneath one was a piece of paper weighted down with Jansen's *Gott Mit Uns* belt buckle. It was a Russian propaganda leaflet exhorting us not to die for Krupp and Siemens.

Even through his hangover, Lüttke was exultant. He crowed, Didn't I tell you? Didn't I tell you? That dirty traitorous Bolshevik bastard. I hope they tie him to a tree and use him for target practice.

Ottermann was so angry he couldn't speak. He started shoving the last of the food back into the satchels as if all this were the food's fault.

Meanwhile Lüttke gloated, wobbling his head from side to side and saying in a sing-song voice, Oh, everyone just blamed old Lüttke, didn't they? But who turned out to be right? Who indeed? It wasn't Lüttke's fault at all, was it? Jansen was just a sneaky little Jew-loving Bolshevik all along.

Once Ottermann had packed up everything except the food near Lüttke's spot, he said, Let's go. If we're lucky, we can still catch him before he hands himself over.

Lüttke said, What do you mean, catch him?

I'm going after him and if you don't want to, you can stay here and lick your own arse for all I care. Meissner, Himmelsbach, are you coming or not?

I don't know why I went along on this fool's errand. In retrospect, that was my opportunity to get out before what happened later. I wasn't under orders and had nothing in particular to accomplish. It wasn't as if I thought we'd find him. I could have gone back to my unit. I could even have acted on what we'd daydreamed, and walked away. I was a few days' hike from Germany, away from my officers with the best food supplies I'd ever seen. There was even a horse.

But somehow, I didn't seriously consider it. I never did desert. I was still following orders when I was finally captured, in April 1945, near Linz in Austria. I suppose I just couldn't really believe in the possibility.

And I'd grown so used to having tasks to carry out that I couldn't understand this widened field of choice. The way I construed the decision wasn't: what of all possible things do I think I should do now? It was: should we go after Jansen? And we did. Lüttke griped about it, of course, but I don't think he wanted to be on his own.

The part of me that still had access to that kind of emotion did feel sorry for Jansen. He was unlucky to arrive inexperienced just when our losses were getting so deep. And I had no faith in the Russians' leaflet. We and they sometimes kidnapped each other's sentries for information, and I'd seen the worst things done to them.

We hastily loaded our food satchels onto Ferdinand. Ottermann and I tried to stitch together a guess at where Jansen would have headed: away from our own unit and in a curve around the Feldgendarmen's hunting lodge to where we'd heard there was a large concentration of Russian troops. Lüttke told us our guesses were worthless shit. He was right. But we had nothing better, so off we went, hurrying unwittingly towards what I first intended to tell you about.

We'd been going for perhaps an hour, Ottermann slightly ahead, drawing us forward, and Lüttke dawdling just enough to register his protest, when we heard a truck engine through the trees. We couldn't see it, but it was one of ours, moving from right to left across our heading. The knowledge that we were fugitives came upon us and we took cover on the ground. Lüttke was lying there still holding the end of Ferdinand's rope.

The horse's ears had pricked up, like two velvety shells, and swivelled to track the engine's movement. I stared at the reddish-brown pine needles in front of my nose and prepared myself to fire and move if the engine stopped. It didn't. And after its mechanical throbbing had dwindled below the level of hearing, we slowly stood up again. Lüttke stroked the horse's nose and told him, You didn't make any noise, did you, my boy?

We crept forward, weapons raised, until we found what the truck had been driving on: a dirt road between the trees. It didn't seem to have been bulldozed, so it had probably been there since before we arrived.

There had been a lot of military traffic. The road surface had been stirred up and mixed with fresh dark dirt from underneath. I could see the tread patterns of troop transports, dispatch riders, jeeps, pony-drawn *panje* wagons and half-tracks. No tanks, though, presumably because we didn't have any left.

Ottermann looked along the road to the right, eastward, then turned back the way we'd come, judging something. He said, This'll be the track that led out of the – whatever it was, the depot, we found yesterday. We must be west of it.

Himmelsbach said, Do you think so?

Yep.

Hadn't we better get off it then?

Yep.

Hold on, said Lüttke. If there's traffic on this road, they'll have picked him up already. Your turncoat Bolshevik friend is so stupid he'll have walked straight into them. We can give up this whole thing.

Ottermann seemed weary. He didn't really try to disagree with Lüttke, just said, He's stupid, but he's not that stupid. I don't think he would have—

Wait! said Himmelsbach. Do you hear that?

We listened. It was the sound of another truck. Quickly we went to hide among the trees again. But before we could get off the road, Ottermann whispered with pain in his voice, Oh shit! Ferdinand's footsteps are all over the road.

The pony had left big hoofprints the shape of frying pans in the loose soil. They came out of the woods, shuffled around and went back in.

Lüttke spoke in fright: Kick them over, we can cover them up.

Ottermann said, What are you talking about?

The noise of the truck was coming closer.

I said, There's no time. Get off the road.

There was no other choice. We rushed into the trees and lay down. I squirmed my elbow into the spongy moss to make a stable rest for my rifle, and sighted along it. The engine spluttered steadily, getting louder. I instantaneously decided that if anything happened, I would not fire. The men in the truck would be our people, not Russians. I had no duty here. If the truck stopped, I would run. Every man for himself.

I noticed Himmelsbach put down his rifle. He rolled onto his back and closed his eyes.

The noise of the truck reached where we'd been standing. Through the cross-hatched branches, I could see fragments of a big shape moving along. I closed my eyes as well, not wishing, just waiting.

The truck didn't stop.

Well, said Lüttke, hurray for the vigilance of the German *Landser* [squaddie].

He made a laugh, but it wasn't very persuasive. Ottermann shifted on to his side. He said, I wonder what they're doing, heading west in daylight on this little road. Maybe emptying the depot.

Something I'd unconsciously registered articulated itself to me. I said, You're right. And it's strange of them not to be driving together. They must be less worried about ambushes than about planes.

Ottermann asked, Have you heard any though?

No. Nothing. Have you?

Ottermann shrugged and said, Not at all.

Himmelsbach said, Maybe they know something we don't.

I said, Yes. Or maybe one of them just fell behind.

We stayed lying on the ground. The trucks had driven straight through our little plan to find Jansen and made it look as flimsy as a film set. In practical terms, it was impossible that we'd be able to find a lone figure erring around the Eastern vastness, even if – even if – there were so many even ifs.

I pinched up a few pine needles off the ground and rubbed them between my fingers. Jansen was drifting from the category of the living to the lost. I thought: poor Jansen, his being there probably hadn't contributed a single iota to the war. Then, inhumanely soon, I noticed that I was getting hungry again. My stomach must have been opened up by all the food.

After a while in which each of us rested inside his own head, Ottermann's conscience must have nudged him.

Without much belief, he said, Come on then. If we're going to catch him, we'd better get moving.

Lüttke said, I bet you whatever you want the Feldgendarmen have got him already.

Ottermann didn't object, so Lüttke went on, And with that Bolshevik leaflet in his pocket, I'm sure he's already swinging from a branch.

No one said anything for a minute. Then Ottermann jerked upright in an angry flinch. He said, Jesus Christ, shit on this whole thing. He might have got through if he'd kept his head down, the stupid shitting idiot. And if *I* get through this, I'm going to find his mum. Hamburg's on my way home anyway. I'll tell her a heap of shit about her boy. And if she wants to, and if the farm is still there, she can come live with us. There's always food on a farm and she'll be welcome.

He seemed settled by this, albeit still irritated, as if he'd come to an unsatisfying agreement with himself.

But then Himmelsbach said, I just hope that, if the Feldgendarmen did get him, they didn't ask him any questions first.

There's a particular sensation when you see death pick your number. You feel it when you're caught in the open by a strafing fighter plane and it banks to fly straight at you; when you're in a foxhole and you hear the shouts of *Urrah!* coming from behind your lines; or when a predatory tank belches out of cover, close enough for you to see into the dark mouth of the barrel as it comes around. It must be what roadkill has time to feel in the second before it's hit. In that instant, all you think is: I'm dead.

Jansen knew our names, which unit we'd come from. The Feldgendarmen could just drive over and pick us up. And our families . . .

Lüttke went out of control with rage. He stormed to his feet and started swearing, That shitty traitor, that Jew-loving Bolshevik snake, that shitty back-stabbing son of a whore.

Casting around for something to punish, he spotted Ferdinand. Lüttke snatched a stick up off the ground and, yanking the bridle rope taut around his fist, thwacked the pony in the ribs.

Our remaining self-control snapped. Ottermann and I both went for Lüttke in fury, bellowing. Placid Ferdinand hawed and whinnied, and reared up on his hind legs, jerking Lüttke forward. His sharp hooves pawed the air like a boxer's guard and Lüttke hit the pony again, whacking the branch across his muscled chest. Ottermann reached them before I did and – finally – punched Lüttke in the head, a clumsy right hook that clipped him below the ear.

Lüttke went over, knocked off balance rather than knocked out, and Ottermann snatched the rope out of the air. He immediately began shushing the horse, speaking softly, calming himself down as well. I was left standing there, my fury still charged. I thought Lüttke might shoot Ottermann from the ground, and I would shoot him if he tried.

I aimed my rifle at his chest, every muscle clenched. I would have killed him. If things had gone on as they were, we would have begun to kill each other or ourselves within a couple of days. But for the time being Lüttke didn't come up fighting. If anything, being punched seemed to have temporarily simmered him down. Now he was just surly. He took off his helmet and rubbed the side of his head while Ottermann spoke to the horse.

Lüttke said, You sucker-punched me. Try that again and I'll murder you.

Ottermann didn't respond, just hushed Ferdinand, whose hooves were still skittering about, and patted his neck.

Lüttke kept talking: You've always wanted my horse. You Communists always want what belongs to other people. But he's mine. And I'll do whatever I want with him.

Despite this assertion, Lüttke didn't try to take the horse back, just kept rubbing the side of his jaw. He said, I wouldn't be surprised if you planned this with your friend, to bring us over here. Probably wanted me to get killed so you could take the horse, didn't you?

Ottermann was still paying attention only to Ferdinand. Lüttke went on, muttering almost to himself: Sad, really, how low people will stoop to try and trip you up. People you thought were your comrades. It doesn't matter how much you give, how much you sacrifice. It's the ingratitude, that's what's sad about it. But I'm not just going to lie here. I'm going to get back on my feet, aren't I? Because that's how we do it. Back on the horse. Ha ha ha.

He stood up, shifted his jaw from side to side, and told Ottermann: Do that again and I'll cut you in your sleep. And you, Meissner, you can put your rifle away. Or are you going to murder a fellow soldier?

I lowered it. I truly had no idea what we were going to do. My diligent schoolboy's instinct rose in me: I thought I might turn myself in and use that to request clemency for my parents and sisters. They would hang me. But perhaps that was now the best result still possible.

Then, to my great surprise, Lüttke said, Alright, we've got to go and see if they do have him. Because if they do, we can't go back to the company. He'll tell them whatever they ask.

Perhaps Lüttke didn't have enough self-awareness to be capable of despair. I could see that Ottermann was surprised too. He looked at me and shrugged his big shoulders helplessly.

I said, Yes, well, what else can we do?

Ottermann said, We're going to die in this shithole of a country. Yes we are. And if I'd lived my whole life and never been to Poland, that would have been absolutely fine by me.

Lüttke took this as agreement, and it cheered him up. He said, That's right, Ottermann, we've invaded a shithole and now we're living in it. Funny, isn't it? But don't worry, uncle Lüttke will sort this out. You just keep punching him and stealing his things, and he'll keep sorting out your mess. That's the sort of man he is. You just be careful with that horse.

Neither wanted to turn his back on the other. So they started warily walking abreast, a few metres apart and parallel to the road. Himmelsbach hadn't moved. He was still lying down and I saw that he was crying again. I said, Himmelsbach, we're going.

I think I'm going to stay here actually.

Come on, get up.

I don't care. I really don't care any more. If you want to leave the horse, I'll look after him.

I went over, put out my hand for him to take and said, Come on, up you get. We've got to see about Jansen.

He rolled his eyes, and said, What the hell do I care about Jansen?

I know. But come on, let's get it over with. Up you get.

He closed his eyes and sighed, acquiescing. Eyes still closed, he said, Fine, fine. Why not? What's one more pointless walk in the woods?

I know, I said and helped him up.

Maybe Jansen had the right idea.

I don't think so.

No, neither do I.

And so off we blundered, close to despair and fearful of each other. What we found, I realise now, I've long bracketed out of my memory, as if it didn't quite happen, or I didn't quite see it.

A few weeks ago, I asked one of the staff here – Martin, you might have met him – to help me find out what became of Jansen. The National Information Office in Berlin keeps a record for every German soldier in the war, telling the ends of their stories in the categories of military thinking: KIA, MIA, invalid, captured, executed. I think that must cover everybody.

Martin's a bit older than you, in his mid-thirties I'd say, with blond hair down to his shoulders like a leftover hippie. A gentle, friendly man, a carer by disposition. He sometimes works in the restaurant at lunch and comes over to chat. We originally started talking because he commutes from near our old village, and he keeps me up to date with what's going on there.

Poor Martin, when he understood what I was asking for his help with, went all stiff and embarrassed. It must have been like going into someone's apartment and seeing a shelf of books about the Third Reich. It makes you wonder. And now I think Martin half suspects I'm one of those old men the news always says have been 'living quietly'. The ones you see being trundled into court with their respirators, trying to look as decrepit as they can.

To be fair to him, there's at least one person here, one of the other residents, who I prefer to stay away from. There's something about the way I've heard him insist that things weren't all bad back then – it makes me wonder why he feels the need, and what he says in private. But in all honesty, if you peel back the layers of acceptable opinion, it's not so rare to find an ugly nostalgia for the days when Germany was for the Germans. Certainly not so rare as our collective shame should make it.

Martin was too polite not to help me. But we sat silently beside each other in the computer room while he worked the keyboard. Anything he had to ask, he said so quietly I could hardly make it out. But I wasn't ashamed in front of Martin. More annoyed, if anything. The cartoonish things he was imagining didn't touch the reality. The only pang came when, in the online form, we had to state my relationship to Jansen. I said that we'd served together, and I'm sure both Martin and I thought about precisely what I'd acted in service of.

Fortunately I paid for the records to be sent by post, so

I didn't have to keep asking Martin to help me check the computer. In the letter, there was a lot of extraneous clutter – addresses for veterans' associations and so on – and what they could tell me about my question was just a few words: Uwe Jansen, missing in action, October 1944.

Maybe he was killed trying to give himself up, maybe he worked in a mine or a Siberian prison camp till he died. Or maybe, after it was over, they let him move to East Germany under an assumed name and he's still there in Prenzlauer Berg or Treptow, a creaky-kneed old Communist watching Berlin turn into a tourist town. I hope so, but it doesn't seem very likely.

I actually never was captured by the Russians. I was captured by Czech partisans, in Austria, near Linz. I think I said that already. We were quick-marching West under humane orders to try and find an American to surrender to before the Russians caught us. Whole armies were doing the same, while the Russians gunned them down from tanks and planes and jeeps. In those last weeks, with the army finally disintegrating, it was less a war than a shoot.

We were so grateful to the Americans for coming. I still am. With the Brits, French, Russians and so on, it felt as if we were locked into another cycle of a rancorous family vendetta. But the Americans, those farm boys from Kansas or Ohio, hardly even knew where Europe was. They saved half of Europe and three-quarters of Germany from the Russians. Our troops in the West shouldn't have fired at them. They should have laid down their weapons, greeted them like brothers and said, Hurry on to Berlin, our Eastern armies will hold back the Russians as long as they can. But of course we fought them, our liberators.

After the war, the fantasists, the retrospective rationalisers, said the Western nations should be grateful to us, because the Russians would have invaded Europe either way, and we held them back long enough for the Americans to arrive.

∼

Callum: In the early 1970s, my grandparents signed up to an initiative by the US armies occupying West Germany to put relations on an even friendlier footing. Every other week, a jarhead from the nearest garrison would come to their house for Sunday lunch. He was called Hal and he was one of those Midwestern farm boys my opa mentions.

My grandparents always claimed that when Hal first came to them, they had to show him how to eat with a knife and fork. Can that be true? I have no idea. Apparently he was also barely literate. My oma, in particular, got very attached to him as a result. She thought he was a benighted soul, one rung of culture up from a grunting troglodyte. She knitted jumpers and scratchy socks for him, and was deeply proud that he had some German-Mennonite ancestry. What Hal made of all this is lost to history.

∼

We were on a country lane in Austria, jogging between flat brown fields speckled with spring green, when some armed men came out of the woods in front of us. Since they were to our West, we wrongly assumed they were forward units of the American Army and gladly surrendered, thinking we'd reached safety.

The Czechs stripped us of our watches, rings and remaining food, and had us start digging the grave they were going to shoot us into. That was when I had to relinquish the watch with the 'love your enemies' inscription my father had given me.

These partisans were used to their work. They had a couple of German lorries daubed with the Czechoslovakian flag and crammed with booty. Some had wristwatches all the way up to their elbows, like barbarian arm-rings.

This was the time when the ethnic Germans living in Eastern Europe, from up by the Baltic down through Poland and Hungary to as far south as Yugoslavia, were being murdered in droves as they tried to make their way to the West. That so many were killed for revenge – nowadays they say half a million people – is something no one spoke about for a long time. What to do with the millions of refugees who did make it to Germany was a big political question in the Fifties. But it was never really a moral question. We had no right to complain about what they'd suffered, or about ethnic cleansing; we wouldn't have had the nerve.

We did it first, and worse. In war, the mechanism of justice is retribution. Woe to the conquered. And justice was performed in aggregate, not for individuals. Each of us thinks, *I* didn't set up the Nazi Party, *I* didn't declare war on anyone, *I* didn't deliver people to the camps. But *we* did.

If it hadn't been for the crimes, we could at least have suffered with pride – a belligerent, war-mongering pride, but pride nonetheless. As it was, we'd come to understand, or I'd come to understand, that we were in the wrong. We had that knowledge hammered into us with the deaths of friends and the rape of our families. And the enormity of our crime meant we had to accept that the punishment, though terrible, was not unjust.

Anyway, my God, as my father would say, my God, that's not what I wanted to tell you about. This is supposed to be a happy part of the story. But let me just say once: woe is right. What a terrible time it was. Thanks be to something that it's over, to some blind mechanism of history or perhaps to some faint indestructible human instinct towards goodness.

And things are different now. The German exodus from Eastern Europe seems to have become an acceptable conversation. I see it mentioned on television, in documentaries, and the people talking about it don't appear to be mad-eyed irredentists.

What's changed is that it's now acceptable for Germans to talk about suffering. And people want to hear about it because they believe there is a connection between suffering and truth. In my experience, at least, suffering shows you the world minus the self-obsession everyone is born with – the assumption that you are the centre of something, that the traffic lights will turn green if you are good, or red if you are bad, or if you are being tested, or being treated unfairly, or whatever explanation you invent.

Suffering made me understand that the traffic lights are

random. It showed me what life looks like when not distorted by hope, or pinned in shape by laws: a vast teeming featureless crowd where some suffer and some have happy lives, and there is no reason.

I know some people drew different conclusions. Himmelsbach for one. But to be candid I think that was a sign of his mental weakness. What it taught me is that there is no right and wrong but what we decide to live by, and no 'fair' except what people effortfully construct. And, lastly, it's all so, so fragile. Governments, banks, cities and houses, it's all so much more fragile than you would believe, as easily blown away as dandelion seeds in the breeze.

But what am I saying? I'm going off track. I was talking about the partisans and the pit they had us dig. While we were still shovelling, two Russian motorcycles arrived. The Red Army had finally caught up with us. The riders conferred with the partisans and essentially said: we're not shooting them any more, we're sending them back to Russia to work.

So I can truly say that the Red Army saved my life. Isn't that marvellous? When they made us sit on our hands and wait to be marched off, I just laughed and laughed.

In the weeks after I was captured, I felt light and open and free in a way I hadn't since I was at school. The whole journey back to Russia I was in a good mood. I watched the charred countryside through the slits in the cattle wagons they moved us in and offered sincere prayers of thanks that it was all over. I didn't have anyone to direct them to, but gratitude itself wants to be expressed.

The whole thousand kilometres that I'd retreated on foot, we now travelled in reverse. Whenever we stopped, the Russians showed us newspaper pictures of the death camps and the bombed-out Reichstag with a red flag flying from it. I should have been beyond consoling. Some people were. But the truth is – and I don't say my reaction was right – I was perfectly content. I wanted the journey to go on for ever.

On my first day in the camp – it was to the north-east of the Black Sea, in the Kuban, where the Cossacks come from; the nearest big town was Krasnodar – I got to the front of the food queue and they poured some thin soup onto the trampled ground in front of me. They said that the Red Cross obliged them to give us food, but they didn't have to give us anything to eat it from.

I don't know why they bothered with this ceremony. I suppose these guards were so far behind the front line they hadn't been able to get their share of vengeance. Luckily for me – lucky again – it was a work camp, so there were tools and lumber. The next day I scratched a bowl out of some scrap wood, and then later a spoon. That's what I ate from for the next three years.

[The bowl and spoon survived captivity intact and my opa brought them home when he was released. Throughout the time I knew him, they sat on a high shelf, never taken down, never discussed, but somehow known about. The spoon snapped in the move to the retirement home, but he kept the two pieces. They're now on a shelf at my uncle's.]

By this time, conditions in the prison camps were much

better than they had been. Earlier, the Russians barely had food for their troops, let alone the accursed Germans. And as they grew accustomed to victory, many of the guards became friendlier. I learned some Russian, not just *davai* [hurry up] and *karacho* [OK].

Once the oceanic relief of surrender had drained away, I was gripped by impatience to get home – anxious, fidgeting, pacing, a ready audience for every rumour and a participant in every scheme. I hurried through my work, as if I could speed up the days, and counted them off my calendar. The others would tell me to work slower, because the Russians would just give us more to do, but I couldn't.

And while the years ticked by in the camp, in Germany people's lives started moving again. My middle sister, Regina, finished university amid the ruins in Dresden. My baby sister, Gisela, enrolled. The rubble-clogged streets started to be tidied up, and the buildings rebuilt. The guards told us, sympathetic but stern, that we'd have to stay until every damaged blade of Russian grass had been sewn back together.

But if I'd been released earlier, I would never have met your oma. Her receptionist's contract at the hospital was only for six months. The Russians did me so many unwitting favours in the end. I was unfeasibly lucky, again and again. I passed through the chaos and disaster unharmed, as if some invisible protector had been guiding my steps. In superstitious moments, I've thought that it was your oma, somehow drawing me towards her. These notions must be how religions begin.

[My opa was captured in 1945 and released in spring 1948. The last Germans in Soviet captivity were sent home in January 1956, just over a decade after the war ended. The Kremlin traded the remaining ten thousand prisoners to the West German chancellor, Konrad Adenauer, for something it wanted at the time: renewed diplomatic relations. There's a famous picture of Adenauer coming back from Moscow, which you can see on Google Image. He's giving a press conference at the airfield – there's a microphone stand in the background – and a crowd has come to meet the plane. A tiny old lady in a crumpled hat has dropped to her knees in front of him. Adenauer's embarrassed. He's helping her up and while he's lifting her, she's kissing his hand.]

Some time in 1947, I fell ill. Maybe a long-delayed relapse of the Volhynian fever. And one day they put all the sick prisoners in a couple of cattle wagons and told us we were going to a sanatorium. That was ominous enough, but when they opened the wagons, we were looking out onto empty scrubland. That was the last time I thought: now I'm going to be machine-gunned.

It turned out, however, that what they'd told us wasn't wholly untrue. The things guards tell you never are. We were going to build a sanatorium for Russian officers. It was heavy work, digging foundations, pushing loads of bricks, and most of the others collapsed onto their barrows or gave out in their sleep.

We'd bed down in a shallow trench, jammed close together to keep warm, and sort out the dead in the morning. When we became too few, the Russians would bring more prisoners from other camps, coughers, tremblers, the one-eyed, the disfigured, the limpers and the amputees. They were buried right there among the foundations, something the guards considered bad luck. If the place is still standing, it's probably become a spa hotel.

But all that time, throughout my period of captivity, underneath the exhaustion and the impatience, in my core I was glad. The catastrophe had occurred. We had lost the war. Germany was ruined, occupied, shrunk, divided. Our government had been hanged. We were at the mercy of our captors and conquerors, citizens of a demolished country, children of a shamed people.

And yet I personally had not been machine-gunned. I was no longer fighting for the Nazis. I owed no obligations. I was responsible for nothing but myself. For the first time since winter 1941, when the Blitzkrieg was stopped on the outskirts of Moscow, what I carried within me was not gathering dread but hope – that one day I would be allowed to go home and get on with my life.

That was a long digression. But, well, as I was saying, we blundered through the pine woods in the direction the trucks had gone. More trucks overtook us, all going the same way. Every time we caught the sound of an approaching engine, we lay down and hid. While we pressed our bodies to the ground, Lüttke whispered to us about what he was going to do to Jansen if he'd been caught. Ottermann and I tried to block him out. Himmelsbach lay on his back, looking up at the sky, mentally absent.

Soon the rest of us started looking up as well. We had

spotted what the trucks were retreating from: Russian aircraft in massed formations, big stately fleets of them, passing over us from the East. Stocky Peshka dive-bombers, long cruciform Tupolevs, lightweight Yak fighters that bobbed in the breeze, all their steel bellies gleaming in the high-altitude sunshine. It was one of those sights to make you understand that the war was less about flesh and bone than heavy industry.

There were more and more of them, so many that we had to speak up to make ourselves heard. And as we walked in the shadow of the trees, we began to hear the deep thudding of bombs landing one after the other in what we used to call giant's footsteps.

Ever more bombers reached their targets and the footsteps started to overlap until they became a cacophony, random and relentless, a group of giants stamping down on the humans scurrying about underneath. I'd been under that kind of bombardment before and the sound tapped a slow trickle of fear.

There were no German cities nearby, so they must be bombing the army. That meant this wasn't an air raid, but an offensive. They'd be smashing our positions into the ground before their tanks and rifle brigades flooded forward. I thought maybe it was time to start getting West, Feldgendarmen or no Feldgendarmen.

We heard the artillery start up as well, the barrages landing a few kilometres away. Lots of howitzers and field guns. Back then I could identify the different types by ear. But I wouldn't have needed to: it was the kind of firepower you hardly have to aim, you just obliterate everything above ground.

Another truck overtook us. We hadn't heard it over the noise until it was very close and, when we lay down to let it pass, I could feel little vibrations running through my palms and torso. We listened while the trees trembled and the pine needles hopped about on the soil.

I began to get spooked, being out here in the woods with only a few others. I could feel the homing urge: to get back into the line, to be one among many. But I recognised fear's voice from the many conversations we'd had before, and reassured myself that we were heading West anyway. We kept walking.

When we noticed that we were close to the edge of the woods, Ottermann tied Ferdinand to a tree and we crept forward on our bellies to where things opened out. At the wood's edge was a high deer fence of wooden posts with mesh between them. On the other side was a very large kitchen garden divided up into different sections. Unusually, it hadn't been dug up.

Beyond it were a cluster of working buildings – barns, tool sheds, an estate office – adjoining the back of a big red-brick manor house. It must have formerly been the home of whoever owned the hunting lodge we'd looted the day before.

Feldgendarmen, middle-aged men with comfortable physiques, were rushing around while glancing up at the sky. They were carrying boxes in relays from the house to a row of trucks waiting in the yard. Another Feldgendarme standing in the back of each truck, arranging the boxes that the others heaved up onto the lip of the flatbed.

Next to the trucks was a polished staff car, a Horch with

swooping fenders and wide running boards, which was being crammed with paintings, candelabras and porcelain by two officers in peaked caps and riding boots. One had a small suitcase he couldn't make fit, so he pulled it open and began flinging handfuls of silver cutlery into the back seat.

As we kept looking, what we saw took on the busy horror of a medieval hell painting. But because it was mid-morning on a sunny day, it appeared with the brightness of a double page in a children's picture book – spot what's happening on the farm.

Over by the tool sheds stood a line of debilitated prisoners, Germans. The Feldgendarmen must have been clearing out their brig. One Feldgendarme was measuring out lengths of rope by coiling it around his arm. Once he had enough, he held the rope taut on the ground so his colleague could saw through it with a large pair of what looked like hedge clippers.

Next to them, more Feldgendarmen tied the freshly cut rope around a prisoner's neck and tossed the other end over an iron bar fixed between two of the sheds. Then they heaved him up to where he kicked and wriggled in the air. There were already a few prisoners dangling there, bumping against each other as their ropes twisted and untwisted. The others lined up, not running but waiting.

In a small yard in front of the main barn, a larger group of soldiers was getting rid of the Polish housemaids and labourers. Our men were a mix of Feldgendarmen and troops from a penal battalion, convicted criminals with a red triangle on their shoulder. They were stripping the housemaids and raping them there in the yard, while their comrades capered about pouring bottles of wine over the rapists' heads and onto the women's faces. The dust from the yard stuck to them and clothes were strewn around where they'd been torn off. I'd never actually seen people having sex before and felt a kind of physical revulsion.

Two soldiers were holding the arms of a naked man about the age I am now, certainly in his seventies or eighties, with a stiff white beard that came down to his chest. They forced him down onto his knees, then further forward, and drowned him in a metal bucket. Once he'd stopped kicking and they let go, the bucket tipped over with his head still in it, and the water inside spilled out into a wet shape around his body.

The other soldiers were crucifying the raped women and the labourers against the sides of the barn. The crucified figures, almost joined hand to hand, looked like that home-made bunting where you cut the shape of a person out of folded paper and then pull it out so they're all in a line. In their agony, they arched or writhed slowly against the pain, like pinned frogs.

A group of our soldiers were wrestling a struggling naked girl, raw-boned and strong, a farm girl. When they nailed through her hand, her shriek carried across to us, and we could hear the sharp hammer strokes above the background roaring of the Russian bombardment.

In a reflex of guilt, I thought this might be retaliation for our robbery of the depot. But that didn't make any sense. And as I watched, it was as if cold, heavy mercury were flowing into my veins, so that I could neither move nor speak. None of the others said anything either, not even Lüttke. I felt the earth quivering and just lay there, struck dumb.

The Feldgendarmen gave no indication of stopping. They still had a lot to get through. There were dozens of prisoners and civilians waiting to be killed. And they had begun burning files as well. They were bringing them out in armfuls and dumping them on a bonfire in the yard, which smoked and choked under the weight of paper.

After a while, Ottermann mumbled to us as if his mouth weren't working properly. He said, Away, we've got to get away from here. Come on.

We crawled back deeper into the woods, and once our legs and feet started obeying us again, we ran.

We almost ran straight into a Soviet tank crew. The Russians were much, much closer than we'd realised. I wouldn't have noticed until it was too late; I was just ploughing on madly.

Ottermann saved us. He must have spotted or heard something, and had enough of his wits left to throw himself down on the mossy ground. The rest of us, out of learned instinct, copied him. I was so full of the noise of my heart that it was hard for any sounds to reach me. But as I lay there, I slowly realised that above the bombardment I could hear Russian voices, one in particular. It sounded as if he was berating someone else, and kept being interrupted.

Later on I worked out that the woods we'd been stumbling around in were shaped more or less like a fan. We'd camped in the wider part, towards the bottom, where the hunting lodge was. Now we were at the narrow top, still close to the manor house but through to the other side. The Russians had parked their tank next to the trees.

I put my forehead on the springy moss and felt the far-off explosives. My routines of reconnaissance or retreat didn't start. I just lay there and felt as if I were only just being held together, like a drop of water held by surface tension.

I wasn't thinking clearly. Noises came at me in a jumble. The shells landing, louder than before. The Russian remonstrating incomprehensibly, quite nearby. I thought I could hear a distant fizz of small arms, machine guns.

My mind kept losing its place in what we were supposed to be doing, and noticing other things. The pines around me smelled sharp and fresh, as if the trees were giving off clouds of raw perfume. The bright blue-green moss beside my hand was hyper-clear, as if I were seeing its dense intricate structures through a magnifying glass. And when I looked closer, I saw that each tiny luminous section was assembled of even tinier sections in varying shades of pale yellow and cold blue.

Ottermann whispered at me, Meissner! Meissner! Are you alright?

I turned to look at him. Yes, why?

His dirty, blond-bearded face was taut and adrenalised. He stared at me, then whispered, You three stay here. Don't let the horse make any noise. I'm going to see what's happening.

Got it.

He hesitated, then said, Are you sure you're going to be alright?

Yes, of course.

He seemed to be about to say something more, but decided not to. He began to slither towards the Russian voice, holding his papasha in front of him and pushing himself forward with knees and elbows. I watched his legs working and the soles of his boots scuffing the ground until he went over a fallen log and down out of sight.

I glanced around at the other two. Himmelsbach looked like men I'd seen with combat stress: slack, eyes unfocused, cheeks wet, mind untethered from the present. Lüttke had his bayonet out and was angrily jamming it into position on his rifle. He kept loosening it again and ramming it back into place. When he caught me glancing at him, he almost lost his temper. He said, Stare at me again and I'll stick you like a pig.

I looked away, up past the tops of the trees. A squadron of Russian planes, cruciform Tupolevs, was passing very high overhead, heading home to reload.

I was starting to come back to myself. The unceasing bombardment was beginning to irritate me. But I felt so tired, as if all my glands had been squeezed out and I needed to sleep for weeks and weeks.

Guilt was what I felt, a reflexive response to human horror. I asked myself again whether it could be a reprisal for our looting. And if not for that, then why?

Now I think it was fallacious to ask for reasons. What reason was there for any of the war? In every answer, the logic of the details only disguises the madness of the whole. I do not believe that a historian's analysis can explain what we were doing there in that Polish wood. Versailles, totalitarianism – these are the mechanisms, but they still fall short of why we actually did any of this in the first place. After all, Communism took off everywhere in Europe; Nazism only really in us.

I think part of it was obedience, that we allowed ourselves to be led into the abyss. And I think there was some violence, some psychotic streak, at work. A purist's desire for *tabula rasa*. Some crack in our national psyche that we acted on calmly and methodically, even humanely. I'm sure the Feldgendarmen considered themselves humane for hanging our soldiers rather than crucifying them too.

I thought some muddy version of these thoughts and after some time, I couldn't have said how long, Ottermann crawled back. His nose and cheeks were pink with exertion, and his breath was coming in gasps. He told us, It's a tank crew – a Russian tank crew – they're out of their tank – at the edge of the woods – two of them are throwing up – the others are trying – to get them back in the tank – it's pretty disgusting.

It was a shock to hear that this wasn't just some patrol. Their tanks were already upon us. It was time to move West, and quickly.

But Lüttke said, We've got to attack before they get back in the tank.

Ottermann said, What?

If we let them get back in there, we won't be able to touch them.

Ottermann let out a long sigh like a tyre deflating, the tension leaving him, and laughed once. He said, You want to attack them? Why not? Why not eh? It's the stupidest thing I've ever heard, but alright, alright. Whatever you want.

His mood was so surprising that I caught it too. Why not indeed? I could summon no reason for or against. It was an absurd, senseless idea, and seemed to fit. This was all ridiculous. I said, Yes, why not? We'll have our own private counter-offensive.

Lüttke, however, was animated by vengeful fury. Already he was tying the end of Ferdinand's rope around a branch. He gripped his rifle as tight as if someone were trying to pull it out of his hands, and said, Hurry the shit up. They'll get back in and we'll lose them. Those shitty Jew-loving Bolshevik arseholes. We're going to rip them limb from limb.

I wriggled out of my backpack. Ottermann checked his papasha. And Himmelsbach announced, I'm going to attack on horseback, on Ferdinand.

He didn't look as if he were going to attack anybody. I'd seen faces like his on men going to their deaths, fatalistic, distant, already foreign to this side of the divide. Ottermann raised his eyebrows and said, You're going to what? Well, I suppose you can attack bare naked if you feel like it. But Lüttke's probably going to be difficult about his pony.

Lüttke said brusquely, I don't care. Just hurry up.

Well, well, said Ottermann. Alright then, Himmelsbach, just don't do anything until we get close.

I wasn't sure Himmelsbach had even heard him. He just started lifting the satchels off Ferdinand's back and dropping them on the ground. Ottermann, Lüttke and I began to creep forward. Himmelsbach waited, holding Ferdinand's rope.

Even though we could intermittently hear the Russian's stressed voice, the woods were thick and it felt like a long crawl. I pushed myself steadily forward, slithering around tree stumps and under low canopies of fern. The earth shook beneath me as I pulled myself across it, and the ferns trembled.

Crawling is hard work, and I could feel the heat rising in my arms and chest. I paused to check on Ottermann and Lüttke. They were level with me, sliding forward, silent, heavy and intent. Ottermann nodded at me, and I kept going.

We were close to the wood's edge when I began to catch glimpses of them. They were perhaps thirty metres from us, twenty of them across open ground. Through the misshapen channels formed between overlapping branches, I could see sections of their grease-dark boiler suits moving around. I moved my head from side to side but couldn't see a sentry. I suppose they hadn't thought they were going to be stopped for very long.

I could make out five of them, wearing their padded tanker's hats with flaps coming down over their ears. Although they were clean-shaven, their faces were seamed with black dirt. With their boiler suits and hats, they were blackish from head to toe, like monkeys or coal miners.

One was on his hands and knees, retching and gulping over a lumpy puddle. The one we'd heard remonstrating, perhaps the commander, was standing next to him, grabbing the man's shoulder and trying to pull him to his feet.

Another one was slowly pacing out small circles with his hands on his lower back like a pregnant woman. His face was tilted upwards and he was breathing shallowly as he tried to walk it off. From time to time he said something to the commander that sounded like reassurance.

I could see two more. One came over to the man who was throwing up, squatted down beside him and tried to get him to drink some water from a metal canteen. The last one was a little way off, with his back to us. He was stretching, holding his heel up to his buttock, hopping slightly to keep his balance, and tilting his head from side to side.

Behind them in an overgrown field squatted the crudely angular steel box of a T-34 painted dark green, one of the newer models with a bigger cannon. Even though it had left a doubled trail of churned brown earth, it was strange to see one at rest, like a dozing monster.

The tankers were vulnerable. Lüttke had been right, in a way. I looked across at Ottermann and, catching his eye, tilted my head towards the Russians.

He nodded yes.

I pointed back towards where Himmelsbach must be, then turned my hand over, palm upwards, asking the question.

He waved that away. We could forget Himmelsbach.

But he was wrong. As we inched further forward, moving very carefully now, I heard a crunching, like lots of twigs snapping, from behind us. I looked over my shoulder and saw Himmelsbach mounted on the dumpy pony, his feet dangling comically down the sides, and his hand punching Ferdinand's rump.

He'd fixed his bayonet, and had the blade-tipped rifle jammed under his arm. Ferdinand jerked, whinnied and bucked, but couldn't shake Himmelsbach off, and broke into a noisy shambling run. Himmelsbach was jolted around like a rodeo rider, his helmet bouncing on his head and his bayonet whirling around as he tried to keep his balance.

Small twigs snapped away on meeting his legs and Ferdinand's chest, then Himmelsbach braced himself to break through a thicker branch, whose pieces tumbled about him. When he unbraced, he shifted his rifle into one hand, like a spear. He didn't look in his right mind.

As he smashed past us, I rolled aside for fear of being trampled and, for a moment, saw him from behind: a helmeted figure being thrown around on the back of a squat little pony.

But then we jumped to our feet and sprinted after him towards the Russians. I slipped as soon as I got up, but kept my feet. I heard Ottermann and Lüttke firing. I could feel the strength in my legs from yesterday's meals and found myself yelling the Russian battle cry, *Urrah! Urrah!*

The Russians were astonished. They'd looked up when they heard Ferdinand crashing about. But now when they should have been getting into cover, they froze in confusion. For a couple of long seconds, they goggled at Himmelsbach as at some surreal apparition hurtling out of the woods. The sick one was still on his knees.

As I ran towards them, I didn't fire. Rather than lifting my rifle, I puffed out my chest like a runner breasting the tape, ready for the Russian bullets to tear it open and let out all that was inside. I felt tremendously free.

If they'd been trained infantrymen, they'd have dropped to the ground and picked us off. But they weren't. They fumbled the pistols out of their leather holsters. The one who'd been stretching dashed for the tank. I heard Lüttke screaming in rage and Ottermann's papasha rattling. The tankers ducked awkwardly and fired at us one-handed. A bullet cracked past my head.

Then Himmelsbach was out of the trees and upon them. He yelled, Hiiiiiiiyahh! and barrelled towards the nearest Russian, who dodged away. Himmelsbach lifted his rifle, flung it, missed, overbalanced and fell down hard beside the Russian.

By then Ottermann, Lüttke and I were out of the woods as well. No one had shot me yet, so I dived into the grass and shot the man in front of me once, twice, three times. It was the one who'd been vomiting. I hit him in the arm, then, as the impact spun him around, in the ribs, then in the back as he fell.

I swung the rifle around and shot the one trying to climb back into the tank. Once just above the hip. My second shot missed him as he tumbled backwards.

I swivelled around again to look for a new target. But there was none. All the Russians were down. To my surprise, none of us were. Only Himmelsbach was still on the ground, bruised but not shot.

I stood up and looked at Ottermann, who rolled his eyes. We both grinned and shook our heads. This was all absurd. Then he went to check on Himmelsbach and I went to check on the Russians.

The second one I'd shot was still alive, lying quietly on his back. I could hear him breathing. He was a skinny teenager, two or three years younger than me, not wearing his pistol belt. That must be why he'd dashed for the tank. His face was bloodless under the dirt and a sickly dampness was gathering around the brim of his cloth helmet. A bead of sweat ran down his temple and curved around his cheekbone towards his mouth.

Even before I went on one knee beside him, I could see that my bullet had come out the other side, a piece of good luck from his perspective. If its passage through him had unsealed any of the sticky containers within, he would probably die slowly. If not, he might well survive this wound. At the time, I was not capable of feeling anything one way or the other, but now – weak and futile though my hoping is – I hope he lived.

He stared at me, then up at the sky, then at the others, then back at me. Not frightened so much as dazed. I was about to give him some water when Lüttke said, Come over here. Look!

Beyond the T-34's green steel hull were more overgrown fields, with grasses and stalks of wheat growing out of the bumpy soil. On our left, the fields were bordered by the treeline, which ran forward and then curved away from us. Near the point where the curve turned out of sight, keeping their distance from the trees, was a fanned-out detachment of around a dozen Soviet tanks, heading away from us.

To me they looked like a gang of low ungainly toads waddling across the uneven ground. Puffs of blue smoke bloomed from their exhausts and, now that I was listening, I could hear their engines working.

Walking among them as if among elephants were perhaps thirty or forty riflemen, their infantry support. Later I understood that they were driving around the woods to the manor house we'd just seen. It must have been some sort of headquarters. I'd spotted nothing there that could hold off a dozen tanks, nor even delay them. The Russians would see what was happening.

The Russian I'd shot touched my boot and mumbled, *Vada* [water].

I knelt beside him again and Lüttke came up behind me, kneading my shoulders with combat euphoria. He said, Did he ask for vodka? These shitting Bolsheviks, eh? No wonder they can't get anything done.

I said, They've done for us, haven't they?

Not yet, my little defeatist! Not yet!

The Russian again mumbled, *Vada*. Lüttke bent down towards him and genially blared, *Karacho tovarich, nyet vodka* [OK, comrade, no vodka].

I put my canteen in the Russian's hand, wrapping his fingers around the metal, and looked around for the other two. Himmelsbach had injured his leg falling off the pony. Ottermann was helping him limp gingerly towards us. Ferdinand was standing by himself, cropping grass.

Lüttke exclaimed, Himmelsbach! You belong in a madhouse! Hiiiyaah!

He mimed flinging a spear, shouted Hiiiyaah again, and pretended to unbalance. I couldn't help smiling. To my surprise, Himmelsbach grinned too, shook his head, grinned wider and then started to laugh. Lüttke grabbed him and ruffled the helmet around on Himmelsbach's head, telling him, You're a lunatic! You should be dead!

You should be, Ottermann agreed.

Himmelsbach laughed again and said, Winnetou! Of all things. My boyhood self would be proud.

Ottermann pointed his plaited beard at me and said, It's a god-damned miracle.

I was less amazed than he was. I'd been in the war longer and was more used to the elation after victory, when all things are miraculous. But I laughed with relief and said, We were lucky they were tankers.

Only in wartime would you joke and celebrate while someone lay on the ground beside you with a gunshot wound. We had no interest in him at all. Lüttke said, Alright then, ladies and gentlemen, who wants a ride in a Communist tank?

Ottermann snorted and said to Himmelsbach, At least you can't fall off it.

Lüttke went on, Yes, we're going to take this tank and stick it to those Russians over there.

The notion that we would do something like that seemed, in that moment, like some marvellous prank. A great jape at the Russians' expense. It was as if I'd grown so huge, so Olympian, that human pain, striving, attempts to survive, life, even my own, was so tiny it couldn't help being comic.

Lüttke wasn't sure how to get into the tank. He put his hands on the metal plate above its tracks, got one knee onto it as well, and awkwardly levered himself up.

Himmelsbach said, This is really stupid, isn't it?

Ottermann said yes, and we all laughed.

It's difficult to explain now what I thought we were doing. But right then the consequences seemed so trivial, and the prank so desperately funny.

Ottermann, who'd already climbed up onto the tank, said, What about the pony?

Ferdinand was still cropping grass, gradually moving away from the Russian corpses.

Lüttke said, He'll just have to fend for himself. We've moved up in the world. Bye bye, Ferdinand, toodle-oo.

He waved goodbye to the pony, and the rest of us copied him, waving and calling out our goodbyes. The pony didn't lift his head, and Lüttke yelled good-naturedly, Piss off then, you ungrateful fucker!

I put my hand on the tank's sun-warmed metal, to climb up, and the Russian behind me mumbled something I didn't understand. I unbuttoned my tunic pocket and put some cheese and a tin of anchovies on the grass beside him. I could afford to be generous; it was unlikely we'd be needing any of it.

The others slid down into the tank and I hurried to catch-up. I clambered over the tracks and onto the monster's back, where I could hear their voices echoing up the turret from inside. The sky was boundless above me. Here and there it was busy with little groups of aeroplanes. The world was so vast, and I had seen so little of it. But, not wanting to be left out, I quickly sat on the edge of the hatch and lowered myself inside.

My legs bumped into Lüttke and Himmelsbach's shoulders and arms, and I found myself jammed uncomfortably between them. Even though they shuffled apart to give me some space, I could barely move. From the inside, the tank was a low, gloomy, white-painted metal room, wider than it was high. The walls and ceiling were fulsomely patterned with pipes, switches, fire extinguishers, radio sets, pictures of women, ammunition racks and I suppose everything else the crew owned. It had the fusty stink of men in an enclosed space and I'd already started sweating with the warmth.

Lüttke was so excited he was almost yelling, right next to me: Meissner! You were in the artillery, weren't you, before you ended up with us louts on foot?

Yes, why?

Good. You can be the gunner. Ottermann's driving, Himmelsbach's loading and I'm the tank commander. There's a forward machine gun, but we don't have anyone to man it. Jansen could have done it if he hadn't been a weak Bolshevik backstabber!

Yes, I said. Would have been useful.

Hurry up, Meissner! Hurry up, your seat's right here!

Letting him rag me, I squeezed past, smelling his breath, and slid myself onto a thin metal seat suspended in the turret. Ahead of me, Ottermann was sitting hunched forward, his chest almost meeting his knees, with a hand on each of the two steering levers. He was peering out of the lifted metal flap at the front of the tank. I asked him, Do you think you can drive it?

He said, No idea, and we all laughed again.

To my right, almost like an armrest, was the base of the gun barrel. At the bottom was a grooved steel tongue along which you slid rounds into the chamber. On the other side of it, poor Himmelsbach was hunched over beneath the ceiling, the walls around him fitted with racks of bright brass shells. There was nowhere for him to stand except on another box of shells. I didn't see how he was supposed to lift them out from under his feet, but then I thought it was unlikely we'd get to fire that many rounds anyway.

I tried to quickly figure out the firing mechanism, and realised it was very straightforward. I suppose it had to be worked by untrained peasants put in uniform. To my left was a small handle mounted on a disc; when I turned it, the turret started turning with me inside it, while the rest of the metal room stayed in place. There was another handle in front of me, for elevation. When I turned it with my other hand, the barrel lifted. The trigger was built into the handle. It was that simple.

At eye-height in front of me was a rubber-fringed sight like that on a long-range rifle. Carefully painted onto the wall beside it was what I recognised as a range table, laying out how much the shell would drop over what distance. All this felt pleasantly familiar and reminded me of the early stages of the war. It was satisfying to know that the skills I'd learned were still in there.

Feeling ever more at home, I pulled a short lever on the side of the chamber to check that there was a shell inside. I saw the gleam of brass and pushed it closed again. I put my eye to the sight, which must have been connected to a periscope, and saw a dim, fuzzy landscape with crosshairs floating on top. I could see the tanks, a row of dark blobs driving away from us. Rotating the side handle to turn the turret, I started counting them.

Someone jostled me and, sitting back, I saw that Lüttke was climbing up the inside of the turret. He reached above his head and pulled down the round metal lid that covered the hatch. I don't suffer especially from claustrophobia, but the clang of it shutting touched some animal part of me. The light now came at stark angles from bulbs mounted on the walls in thick wire baskets, and the only passage to the outside was the small forward flap that Ottermann had open. I had to busy myself rechecking the equipment until the claustrophobia passed.

Lüttke, his voice booming oddly in the closed box, said to Ottermann, Close that flap up.

Ottermann said, Absolutely not, and I was grateful to him.

Fine, said Lüttke. He manoeuvred himself onto a seat above and behind me, with his knees bumping my shoulder blades. Fine, he said again: Driver, start her up.

Ottermann rapped his knuckles against his helmet for luck and pulled a lever beside him. The engine rattled and caught, and the floor, walls and ceiling began to shake. The engine clattered like a tractor's, but rose to a higher pitch as Ottermann cautiously revved it up. I wished I'd taken the tankers' ear protectors. Lüttke yelled above the din, Come on then, we're not ploughing a shit-stained field! Let's get after them!

Ottermann's right arm wrestled with a tall gear lever, jerking it awkwardly around until something bit. The tank lurched and my head hit the wall in front of me. My helmet rang like a bell and the engine cut out.

You stalled it, hooted Lüttke. Jesus shitting Christ.

Himmelsbach asked if I was alright. I nodded, feeling my brain shift in its case.

Ottermann restarted the engine and wrestled with the

gear stick again. Gradually, almost imperceptibly at first, we started rolling forward. I glanced at Himmelsbach, who grinned and raised his eyebrows.

Ottermann pressed down on the throttle and we began to pick up speed. The tank felt surprisingly agile. Despite the throbbing in my skull, it was exhilarating. I grabbed the shaking sight and held my eye to it. The dim landscape and the tanks were jumping and plunging as we jounced across the uneven ground. Every screw and buckle and bolt was vibrating. My rear end was lifting off the seat and smacking back down.

Lüttke yelled in my ear, How close do we need to get? So you won't miss?

I guessed and shouted, Two hundred metres!

Even with the tank moving, I couldn't miss from there. Lüttke bellowed at Ottermann, Did you hear that? Two hundred metres!

Ottermann leaned his head back over his shoulder, and yelled, What?

Two hundred metres!

How far are we now?

I shouted, Maybe a kilometre!

Ottermann yelled back, Hit the second one from the end! Then we'll take the end one at close range!

Lüttke shouted, Good idea! Hear that, Himmelsbach? You've got to load fast. I'll take care of the infantry with the machine gun up here.

I knew he'd never 'take care' of a whole company with one machine gun, and that even if we did hit the two end tanks, that would simply leave us in range of ten more.

But Ottermann went up a gear and stamped the throttle; the tank bounded from a jog to a gallop. And my heart answered the engine's call. It was elation, the pure confidence you sometimes get before combat. I felt as if we were buccaneers racing up behind the wallowing merchantmen ahead of us. A children's book fantasy.

And beside me, Himmelsbach shouted, Hiiiiyaaah!

I started shouting, Hiiiyah! Hiiiyah! as well, banging my fists on the wall. And Lüttke and Ottermann were shouting too, curses, whoops, invented war cries.

Lüttke drummed his fists on the wall and began bawling out the rumpty-tumpty marching song *Alte Kameraden*. I joined in, the others too, as loud as I could, bellowing my lungs out in the roaring, pitching box. The song gave shape to my tangled and tremulous feeling, and even if it didn't quite fit, what I felt took that form, ardently:

> Old comrades on the march through the country
> Swear a friendship that's rock-solid and true.
> Whether in need or in danger
> They always stick together through and through.

I held my eye to the sight and tried to estimate the distance to the Russian tanks. My mind was too full to understand the scale on the crosshairs. I guessed and shouted, Four hundred metres!

I could see fewer of them at a time through the periscope, and their fuzziness was resolving into focus: the tanks' angled bodies, the wide exhaust pipes, the men walking among them in uniforms that were greeny-yellow where ours were greeny-grey. The armour plating on the tanks' backs would be thinner than on the front. But none seemed perturbed that we were rushing up behind them. They must have thought their comrades were just catching up.

We kept on singing over the racket and I was suddenly very moved, as if I needed to weep. The slightly stupid chorus seemed deeply poignant and meaningful:

> Laughing, joking, laughing, joking, because
>   today is here today.
> Tomorrow the regiment will be scattered who
>   knows how far away.
> Comrades, we're destined to be parted.
> So grab a glass and shout, Prost!

After all, despite my four years at the front, I was only young, and close to death. And the heart needs a form to put its feelings in.

I put my eye to the sight again. We were now close enough that I needed to turn the turret to get the right angle. Ottermann had us on a heading that would take us past the end of their row. Rotating the handle, I moved the crosshairs past the end tank to the back of the next one along. The crosshairs pitched up and down. The tank got bigger and clearer. I could make out a white number painted on the turret, and the belts and shoulder straps of the infantry. One or two were glancing over their shoulders.

The others kept singing until I guessed again and shouted, Two hundred metres!

Lüttke, bouncing in his seat, yelled at me, Fire then, Meissner!

But our tank lurched over something. The crosshairs dipped, then heaved up into the sky.

Lüttke yelled again: Shit god damn it, Meissner, fire god damn you!

And I fired.

The propellant banged in the chamber, our tank sat back heavily on its suspension, and in the dim periscope landscape I saw the Russians' tank explode. Their turret leaped up vertically like a ping-pong ball on a fountain of flame, then tipped forward over itself. Meanwhile a second, narrower jet of flame and smoke flared out of the ragged hole our shell had punched through the thin rear plating. The five men in there can hardly have known they'd been hit.

Lüttke's machine gun started chattering above me. Stray shell casings tapped me on the shoulder. The Russian formation scattered: the infantry threw themselves down in the long grass. The tanks broke their line, some bucking forward, some wheeling, some throwing themselves into reverse, like fireworks that fly up in echelon and then burst into different directions. Bullets began going ting-ting-ting on our armour.

The end tank, the one we'd isolated, was turning on the spot. Presumably they couldn't see what had happened. The hatch on top was pushed up and a head wearing a tanker's hat popped out. I barely saw him before he pulled the hatch shut again. The tank started reversing as it turned, its tracks grinding in opposite directions and its turret sweeping around towards us.

I pulled the chamber release lever. It clanked open, spraying up a pungent lungful of chemical fumes. I started hacking while the hot shell casing flew out and hit Himmelsbach on the leg. Himmelsbach yelped and shouted, but didn't drop the replacement shell he was bracing across his forearms.

The bullets were now going ting-ting-ting-ting-ting and Lüttke yelled at Ottermann, Close that shitting flap! They're shooting at the flap!

Ottermann, however, was locked on course, as if he were going to ram them amidships. A grenade went off very close to us and we rocked slightly from side to side. Through the periscope I could see the Russians' turret coming around. They were bringing it around faster by spinning the hull as well. The barrel was past ninety degrees, the angle narrowing towards us. I had our crosshairs lined up and I shouted at Himmelsbach, Reload! Reload, Himmelsbach! Reload!

Lüttke was shooting bursts and shouting, Fire! Fire!

Ottermann had the engine at screaming pitch. We were barrelling right at them. I could see their muzzle lowering as their gunner adjusted the elevation. Then Himmelsbach shoved the shell into the chamber and in the same second I squeezed the trigger again.

This tank I hit side-on, more or less at the joint between the body and the turret. The explosion flipped it over like a toy, one track still spinning vainly in the air. Lüttke yelled, Hiiyah! Hiiyah! But I had had enough glee. I was afraid for my life.

Ottermann yanked the left-hand track into reverse. The

metal screeched and the tank cornered at speed, its centre of gravity heeling over. Another grenade hit us. I heard the double thud of two tanks firing almost in unison. The shells must have flown overhead, who knows how close, and both went off on the far side, one so near that earth and pebbles rattled down on our armour.

Ottermann was swerving us in cumbersome zigzags, heading for the cover of the trees. I pulled open the chamber. More chemical fumes. The hot casing clanked on the floor. I pumped the side-crank, trying to spin the turret all the way round to fire backwards, and shouting at Himmelsbach to reload. Then we were hit.

The shell must have clipped the front corner of our tank rather than striking us dead on. In any case, the first I knew about it, everything was sound and I was flying sideways in the dark.

There were very many hard or sharp things to collide with, and the impact knocked the sense out of me. I lay sprawled forward, still in darkness, my body immobilising itself against the pain of movement, with no clear idea of where or who or why I was. I would have lain there until the Russians dragged me out and, presumably, treated me as badly as they could imagine. But Lüttke dragged me out first.

My recollection of how he and Himmelsbach got me through the hatch isn't continuous, as if my brain stuttered while the memory was being written. I remember coughing up smoke; Lüttke and Himmelsbach's hands on me; the light from the hatch streaming in horizontally because the tank was on its side.

I saw Ottermann's body. He'd been sitting closest to where the shell had gone off. It had buckled the armour plating and folded it around him. His head and upper torso were hanging out of it like a flap of ham from a sandwich.

They hauled me out under the enormous sky. The soundscape opened. I wasn't wearing my helmet. I could hear the bombardment in the distance. The tank lay smoking beside us like a hulking windbreak. I could feel scratches and bruises everywhere, as if my suit of skin were tingling. The cloth of Lüttke and Himmelsbach's uniforms was ripped and singed. Lüttke's cloak was torn away, leaving only a kind of ragged neckerchief. One side of his face was crimson, like a costume mask, the blood gathering into droplets on his stubbly mutton chops.

He was bawling at me, Meissner! Meissner! Can you walk? Meissner!

My mind was still putting its pieces back together. Lüttke helped me up. Himmelsbach could hardly stand either. He had all his weight on one leg, the other boot only just touching the earth with its toe.

To my right, across the fields, I could see the manor house where the Feldgendarmen were. The tanks must have been heading towards it.

Lüttke bawled at me, Meissner! You've got to run to the trees!

The treeline was perhaps a hundred metres from us. A ten-second sprint for an athlete on a track. I could see the safe darkness under the pines. I started to hobble, with Lüttke holding me up and Himmelsbach hobbling alongside. Once we got out of the lee of the tank, the Russian infantry spotted that we were alive and began shooting.

Bullets whined and popped past my head, aimed for me. The Russians were too far away to be accurate, but my legs were wobbling and stumbling. The treeline was hardly getting closer. Even Himmelsbach, making an ugly jerky limp, was leaving me behind.

I could feel the sunshine warming the back of my tunic, Lüttke's arm around me like a life-ring, a breeze trailing its fingertips across my face, and I thought: this is my last conscious moment. Any second now, one of these bullets is going to turn out my lights. And I cried while I hobbled, with frustration and self-pity: that I wouldn't see my family again; that I had kept going for so long, for nothing.

But Lüttke – sweating, swearing – carried on pulling me forward. He yelled at Himmelsbach, Fire back at them, you pansy!

He unexpectedly grabbed my arm, crouched and heaved me over his shoulder, my body folding at the waist. He staggered, found his balance, and began lumbering forward. I was looking down at the wild grass. My face jolted against his soaking back. I heard Himmelsbach take a couple of potshots.

Craning my neck, I saw our tank jutting up against the landscape, a wreck of abandoned machinery. One corner was crumpled like a sheet of tin foil squeezed in the fist. The Russian infantry were standing up out of the grass. They must have thrown themselves down when Himmelsbach shot at them.

Further off behind them, a trail of oily black smoke was gushing up out of the first tank I'd hit, and dirtying the sky. At the other, which wasn't on fire, the crew was being carried out. The other tanks were sitting in motionless disarray, presumably waiting for their infantry to mop us up.

Lüttke was wheezing and struggling under my weight. The Russians' bullets were zipping into the grass around and in front of us. I realised that Lüttke was slowing down. After a little further, he leaned forward and pitched me onto the ground. He'd decided to leave me behind after all.

But I was wrong. He threw himself on top of me, covering my body with his own. I had my chin in the soil, with Lüttke above like a very heavy blanket. He started firing aimed shots, one, two, three. I could smell his sour sweat and hear him shouting between big gasps of air, Shitty Bolsheviks – shitty god-damned – Communists!

He was digging the point of his elbow into my back to support his rifle, and I was so grateful I would have lain underneath him for ever.

Then he jumped to his feet and started pulling me up again. The sound of an aircraft engine detached itself from the background noise, and plunged down out of the upper sky. The noise separated and I saw three Russian fighter planes, tiny quick Yakovlevs, as agile and silvery as whitebait, hurtling towards us.

They were presumably on the way home from escorting a bombing run. They must have spotted the wrecked tanks and the infantry, and whatever they thought was going on, they drew the wrong conclusion. They were in a flying V, the two subordinates on the leader's wingtips, about house-height above the grass. They were moving at the kind of speed you can only understand when they're close to the ground. I could see their propellers, the blur around the planes' noses, the cockpits, the thin front edges of the wings. Few things induce panic like an aeroplane flying straight at you. Lüttke pushed me back down again with himself on top, shielding his head.

The Russian infantry didn't take cover. Once the Yaks were very close, their machine guns started twinkling like three pairs of stars, inaudible over their engines, and they strafed their own men. It was like watching sewing machines race across cloth: each gun ripped a line of punctures through the earth, running across the meadow and across the soldiers. I saw one infantryman, in the last instant, raise his palms to prevent the mistake, but the stitches punched right through him. The planes banked, already far away, bringing themselves around for another pass.

Lüttke hauled me upright again, draped me across his shoulders and, gasping and stumbling, carried me to the treeline, where he dropped me. Himmelsbach was limping so badly he had fallen behind, and was trying to use his rifle as a walking stick. Lüttke went back for him.

I crawled behind a tree trunk and saw the Russian detachment falling back in confusion. Someone had let off a magnesium signal flare, an airborne spot bright even against the sunshine. The Yakovlevs buzzed them, this time not firing. But the detachment was already driving back the way it had come, breaking off its advance.

We never found our way back to our company. We headed West, away from the Russians, and the soldiers we met had been scattered into small bands, hiding in the woods and traipsing slowly through the Polish landscape. They and we were all looking for the army, amid a rising fear that we'd been left behind the Soviet advance.

But eventually we found some sentries, some semblance of order, and a field kitchen catering to hundreds of exhausted, injured troops. We ate the millet and cabbage soup, and regretted our lost feasts. From the others we pieced together that our company had been strung out along one of the stretches of front that the Russians had punched their armour through. Rows of tanks must have rolled right over their heads. No one was going to be asking us where we'd been.

As these military offcuts, half a patrol here, the remnants of a battalion there, re-organised themselves, like an ineradicable mutant growth, we were lumped together into a new company with a couple of dozen other castaways. After a few weeks, I was sent to help repair some telephone lines, on the basis that trained artillerymen had 'technical' knowledge, and I never saw Lüttke or Himmelsbach again.

Lüttke's record I looked up at the same time as Jansen's. His first name was Karl-Heinz. He was killed in the new year, in a village in Bavaria, presumably in order to keep it in German hands for an extra ten seconds. He'd got his promotion to *Unteroffizier*, so his widow will have had the bigger pension. Unpleasant as he was, I wish he could have been given a medal for dragging me across that field; he would have liked one.

Himmelsbach, Michael, I saw in the newspaper in the 1960s, not long after we'd arrived in the West. He was writing in *Die Welt* [a bland conservative broadsheet set up by the British authorities after the war] about the effect a new regulation was going to have on small publishing houses. I cut it out and must still have it somewhere. At the bottom of the article, where they put information about the author, it said that Himmelsbach was director of a small art book publisher's in Freiburg, not at all far from us. I didn't take up contact. But I was glad he seemed to have made a success of his life afterwards. He was ten years older than me, so he may well be gone by now.

As for our joyride in the Russian tank, I still can't quite say whether it was an act of evil. We interrupted the Russians on their way to the house that the Feldgendarmen were liquidating, and stopped them from getting there. I don't even know for certain what horrors we allowed to be perpetrated. But I can still hear the sharp hammer strokes driving the nail through that girl's hand. And her shriek carries to me across the decades.

Did we do wrong? By the morality of consequences, yes, undoubtedly. But it's hard for me to accept that so baldly, because by the morality of virtues, of character, the others at least were brave and loyal. And having seen that courage, I don't find it easy to dismiss.

But to say simply that it's complicated is inadequate. And

to say that there are two sides is a theoretician's answer. I have needed something to live by, and to know whether to consider myself a good man.

I've been turning it over for most of my life, and all I've found are more complications: could we even have acted differently without being different people? Shouldn't you judge a crime by how far it deviated from what the times expected? And can you do real evil without meaning to?

These are questions for ministers and philosophers. And sometimes, for years at a stretch, I would say to myself, I was only young; I was doing my duty; I look after my children, I love my wife and I pay my taxes, how can I be an evil man? And yet, we are not talking about some youthful indiscretion.

Finally, after a lifetime, I realise that the kind of thinking I unconsciously inherited from my father, of evil and good, has been unable to provide an answer.

And how I've actually lived is that I haven't rationalised my way to innocence, nor worn sackcloth and ashes, nor ducked the question by saying it's too complex to pick apart. I wear a mark of shame. Over the years I've realised that, instead of trying to wash it clean, I just have to carry on wearing it. No matter what anyone says, it was me who held the rifle, and it always will be. I killed a great many people in the war. I was never close to being one of the era's few heroes, but neither was I one of its butchers or sadists. I was who I was, I lived as I lived, I tried as hard as I tried.

If I were asked to put my life on the scale of justice, the only thing I would set against the war – and this may not make any sense to you – is your oma. I've got no reason to believe that I loved her any more than anyone loves anyone else. But that I was capable of such vast clarity of feeling, that something so good and so totally without self could inhabit me, is the only thing I'd have speak on my behalf. And when it comes down to it, all it is is that I loved her, and I love her still.

What I remember from my life, what sticks with me, is what we began that afternoon in Dresden in 1948, when I was back from Russia and it snowed on the daffodils in the hospital garden. In those few minutes we started a conversation that we carried on until she died. I am still carrying on my half.

I remember how happy she was when she was first pregnant, with her hand always moving unconsciously towards her little pot belly. I remember the first time we went on an exotic holiday, in the 1970s, to New York, and how hard she tried not to seem too excited. We were already middle-aged by then, and still she hadn't wanted to spend the money until I convinced her we could afford it.

It wasn't like today, when people fly off somewhere for the weekend. Just to be in New York at all was a treat of decades. And then to live so sumptuously that we went to a fashionable restaurant, in Manhattan, that your oma had read about in the guidebook. Everyone was younger than us and dressed in black. I remember suddenly noticing the jackets we were wearing, beige windcheaters. Your oma was so thrilled to be there. She didn't get much of a youth, you know. And now here we were, in a restaurant in Manhattan, free and prosperous and at our ease.

I saw her quick clever eyes not looking at me, but glancing around everywhere, trying to memorise the decor, the food and the people. I don't remember any of it except her – her eyes that I'd already known for more than half my life, and how happy she was.

That mattered to me, matters to me now, more than anything: more than the war, more than anything I did or didn't do, more than the question of what kind of man I am. That may not be a moral answer, but it's the truth.

~

Callum: It's getting harder for me to picture my oma. She died when I was still at school, getting on for twenty years ago. The time when she was still alive, the German part of my childhood, is receding ever further into the past, a lost world. I've got no reason to visit the retirement hotel in Heidelberg any more. And I'm the oldest person able and willing to remember: my mum has a chronic illness and can't tell any stories; my dad doesn't want to be reminded of a painful divorce.

These days I just live in London, doing London things. Sometimes I have dreams that my grandparents are alive, my mum is well again, and we are all back in their big brown flat above the pharmacy. I can hear the timbre of their voices, I can speak to them again, and I tell them how much I've missed them.

But in the waking world, it's all gone. I actually witnessed one ending of the long conflict that began in 1914 and rolled on via Versailles, Stalingrad and Berlin, until the Wall came down in 1989. It was at night in what I guess was 1991. I would have been five, staying at my grandparents' in their village. We were woken up by a terrible mechanical screeching and the roar of engines. My oma, who'd recognised the sound, came into my room to keep me close. I asked what it was and she said, *Panzer*. A sleepy little kid, I thought, *Panthers?!*

We went out onto the balcony and saw a column of American military vehicles, tanks, rocket launchers, troop carriers, driving along slowly under the streetlamps. The next morning, all the customers in my opa's pharmacy complained about the potholes the caterpillar tracks had left in the tarmac. And the local news reported that the troops were retreating from their stations on the inner-German border, between east and west, a line that had been rubbed out.

After my oma died, my opa lived and lived. At the time, I thought I was a pretty good grandson, turning up for a week every couple of years. Now that I'm married, I'm starting to get an inkling of how lonely he must have been. All those quiet afternoons on his own, doing crosswords, watching the news. He kept on going to the bakery in the mornings, reading *Die Welt*, heading out with his walking group, on into his nineties.

He got smaller, his hair purer white, his walks shorter. In his last few months, the bright circle cast by his mind began to shrink into itself. It took him a while to sort through who everyone was. His legs grew weaker, he started to need a wheelchair. And one day when he was being wheelchaired to the in-house restaurant, his head fell forward on his chest, and his loneliness ended.

As for me, I'm forgetting how to speak German properly. But my ear still picks up resonances that my British-British friends don't hear: black bread, *Schlagermusik*, echoes of central Europe. My wife's pregnant now for the first time and wants me to teach German to the child, like my mum and grandparents did with me. I'm going to try, though it's all a generation further away.

And I wonder whether any of this, this conflicted inheritance, will mean much to someone born in London in 2020 to British parents. As I said, so much is lost. I just hope that my grandparents' world wasn't razed to the ground, but ploughed under, like clover is to enrich the soil. And I hope that caught somewhere between these pages is an echo of my opa's voice, for my children, and my children's children.

Acknowledgements

My thanks to Anna Webber, Mark Richards and Ben George. Also to Candia McWilliam, without whom this book would not be what it is. And with love to Stella, my first and dearest reader.